DEI

By the same author

THE POMEGRANATE TREE
THE HEART IN THE CASKET
WOMEN OF A CERTAIN AGE

DEIRDRE KINCAID

COLLEEN KLEIN

C

CENTURY

LONDON MELBOURNE AUCKLAND JOHANNESBURG

*All the characters in this novel are fictional,
all settings imaginary*

First published in Great Britain in 1988 by
Century Hutchinson Ltd
Brookmount House, 62–65 Chandos Place,
London WC2N 4NW

Century Hutchinson South Africa (Pty) Ltd
PO Box 337, Bergvlei, 2012 South Africa

Century Hutchinson Australia Pty Ltd
PO Box 496, 16–22 Church Street,
Hawthorn, Victoria 3122, Australia

Century Hutchinson New Zealand Limited
PO Box 40–086, Glenfield, Auckland 10,
New Zealand

ISBN 0 7126 1959 3

Printed and bound in Great Britain by
Anchor Brendon Ltd, Tiptree, Essex

To Douglas Stewart

1

She sat in the chair shaped like a throne and watched with her dark and guarded eyes while her husband bounced out of his companion chair and shouted for silence. Thrones, he had called them. Look at that purple plush, Deirdre, and you'll see there's no other name for them. They're a present for you. Long as I live I'll never stop bringing you presents, love. That was Reggie, always blathering.

Now he had quit his chair for the place he liked best of all, the place in the limelight. Old as he was, and knocked-about, his hair more grey now than sandy, his teeth dropping out at the rate of one a year, he still had to be up there, footing the bill and running the show.

Deirdre Kincaid looked them over, all the wedding guests who meant nothing to her, nothing at all. Even her stepson, Hugh, she'd never set eyes on him till this day, his wedding day. A lovely boy, Reg had kept saying, for a year or more he'd said it over and over. Wait till you get a look at my boy Hughie, you'll see for yourself.

Reg was right, she thought, the pictures never did him justice: they showed how tall, but not that way of moving, not the glossy brown skin, either. She watched him now while he watched his father.

Catching her gaze, Hugh Kincaid turned his head and smiled at her. The whitest teeth he had, square and even. No wonder Reg loves him, she thought, deeply sad for no reason she could name. Maybe it was being young she was mooning after. She smiled back at him, then turned to the rest of the gathering. So many of them there were, too many to sort out, so many young couples looking like the ones to the right and the left of them, all dressed the same way. They all ran together in her mind.

Reg was in his element. He had got to the reading of the

telegrams. Somewhere along the line he'd turned into master of ceremonies as well as host.

"If there's one thing I hate it's these dirty telegrams," he was roaring over the din. "Here's one from America, Hughie. Maybe this one'll have a bit more class." He opened it and read it aloud. "Nice guys finish last."

The guests collapsed with laughter, repeating the words and slapping their knees. Sheila, the bride, was pretending to be embarrassed. The day she's embarrassed, thought Deirdre Kincaid, that'll be the day. She's been on the job since she was fourteen or so, that one, and the boob she's got hold of, he thinks he's the first. Her eyes travelled again to Hugh. Yes, I reckon she's the first girl he ever had, so he thought it his bounden duty to take her to church.

How hot it was in here, noisy as the fun park on Boxing Day, noisier. She felt her head swim, and the faces, as she blinked, blurred before her. Somehow Reggie had squeezed in half a dozen small tables and twenty hired chairs, and set them all up in front of the long trestle where he'd arranged the ones he called the V.I.P.s: himself, that went without saying, the bride and groom, the bride's mother and stepfather, and one more, the bridegroom's stepmother. Deirdre eyed them, the rest of the V.I.P.s. New stepfather, by the antics of him, his eyes licking over his fat wife. No doubt there's someone for everyone, she thought: a more terrible-looking pair I've yet to see, both of them pleased as Punch to be in on the party without having to pay for it.

Reg was up to his twentieth telegram. "Number twenty," he called. "This one's from Toby Beggs, the best coach in Australia, bar none. I used to work with him in the old days at North Sydney, before he got his own set-up." No one was listening to him, all too busy swilling and guzzling. "Quiet!" he bellowed, quick as usual to fly into a paddy. "Or I'll turf you out into the street, the whole bloody lot of you!" The noise died away, or most of it. He read. "Here's hoping for another Olympic champion nine months from now.—What about that, Hughie?"

Now Reg was chuckling, for some reason the telegram tickled him. "We might beat them to it, eh Deirdre?"

Deirdre looked down at the table, wet with wine. Whenever he was liquored up Reg acted like Casanova. Must have been terrible for him when that fight loused him up; barring that he'd have gone on till eighty, a gutsy little bloke like that. Not that I'd have been on the receiving end, no way.

"Hey, wait on! We might get in first!" hollered Sheila's mother. "Remember I've just turned forty. Life begins at forty, as the saying goes." Beads of perspiration ran down her cheeks and she mopped them up with a handkerchief doused in scent. Four rows of pearls adorned her chest. Her dress was cut so low it nearly showed her navel. She lifted up her double chin, braying like a donkey. Her bit of a husband, not half her size, gave her arm a love-pinch. Just as well the weight goes that way, thought Deirdre, else she'd be squashed flat by morning.

The telegrams had had their day. Done with, they were shoved into an untidy pile, then knocked to the floor. The hired waiters were flat out, first serving the fruit salad and ice-cream, then bringing in the buckets of champagne, with the necks of the bottles sticking out. All the young couples were restless, they had been kept sitting still too long. Everyone had finished with the fruit salad bar Jacky Mobbs: he was Reggie's best friend, so he thought he was privileged, refusing to give up his plate till he'd tilted it up and scooped out the last morsel.

Tiger Bennett, the other old bloke from Reggie's past, down from Woop Woop or Woolgoolga or God knows where—no, Cooktown it was, he'd taken his suit out of moth-balls for the occasion: the smell blew across the table every time he reached for another beer. His wife had put henna in her grey hair, then had a go at brushing it up into a pompadour. They were sitting close together, sharing some joke. She pretended to smack his face. He showed a double row of false teeth that stretched from one big red ear to the other. Wait till you see Tiger, Reg had kept saying, he's got a smile like a slice of watermelon. So now she'd seen him.

The young ones were prettier by far, being young, but no less drunk. No doubt it'll be like the ball at Kirriemuir, she thought, half-amused, half-revolted: from Belfast to Sydney, it's always the fitting end to a wedding.

Reggie was on his feet again, his voice hoarser, but not giving up on it. "I ask you all to be upstanding and drink a toast to my son Hugh and his bride Sheila." He stopped, had a think and started again. "Also to her newly-married parents." He was put out by the hoots of laughter, then he took credit for his slip of the tongue, making out it was what he meant to say. "In passing, I want to make mention of my son's Olympic medals and the way he represented his country overseas, both at the Games and his university career in America. He mightn't want to brag about the medals he brought back, but I tell you this, his old father'll never forget that time. Specially as I had a hand coaching you, eh Hughie?" He winked at Hugh, who ducked his head, really shy, not just putting it on. "Alright, I won't make you blush. But a better son never walked the earth, and now he's got himself a fitting mate in Sheila, his lovely little bird, I mean bride. We're all rooting for you, Hughie."

"Keep it clean, you old bugger!" shouted Tiger.

Reggie froze. "What did I?—Oh listen Tiger, you're the only bloke with a mind dirty enough to think—You watch yourself boy, you just watch yourself—" He stopped glaring at his old mate, but his fists stayed clenched. "Up you get, all of you! I ask you all to charge your glasses and drink to a long life and a merry one together. To Sheila and Hugh."

They all got up, somehow or other, some of them nearly tipping over. They all drank.

"Wow, what a party!" called Ben, Hugh's friend.—Another swimmer, was he, Deirdre wondered: he had the same build as Reggie's boy, brown as a berry, too. His girl-friend was the spitting image of Sheila, red-headed though, not blonde.

They might as well all put their trotters in the sty and be done with it, pigs have got better manners, she thought to herself, turning her lips up in a smile and saying nothing. Now the cake was cut by the two of them, with Ben taking pictures nineteen to the dozen.

One by one they pushed back their chairs and went to squash into the other room, no bigger than this one, but with less in the way of furniture. Timmy had brought his guitar, like Reg he was always glad of a chance to perform. He'd been working for them the year they'd had the lease, and Reg reckoned he'd never put on a better bloke. Short in the legs though he was, Timmy, with a pushed-in mug, he had no trouble getting his pick of the girls, always good-looking and mostly tall, like the one he was cuddling now, one arm round his guitar and the other round her waist.

Be hard to resist him, thought Deirdre, there'd be no stopping him, he'd get up on stilts if needs be to kiss the girl of his choice. More like Reg than his own son, that quiet one over there, pulling Sheila's chair back, keeping his tongue still and his hands to himself. Takes after his mother, I suppose, the one that ran off with the little girl, leaving the boy behind her. Some women, they don't know their luck. Reg wouldn't hear a word against her, though, he'd given her a lot to put up with, he said. Then he'd shut his mouth like a trap, and the subject was closed.

Tim had boned-up a lot of old love-songs. "Ramona, I hear the mission bells above," he was singing; the next moment he'd forgotten it and changed over to The Pagan Love Song. He forgot that, too, but it didn't matter, nobody was listening.

"Here's one for you, Deirdre," he sang out, coming across to her side. As usual he started halfway through. "She stepped away from me and she moved through the fair," he sang, making calf's eyes at her.

"Don't sing that Tim!" said Deirdre, sharply.

"I learned it for you." He looked injured. "It's the one I think of whenever I see you down the park."

Deirdre shook her head. But Sheila had her ears pricked.

"Sing it for me, Timmy," she wheedled him. "I want to hear it."

Timmy looked from one to the other of them. "Sorry, Sheila, I've forgotten how it goes."

Deirdre felt pleased. It wouldn't be too often that girl was crossed. But then why wouldn't Tim want to please the boss's wife, I'm his bread and butter, or at least married to his bread and butter.

Sheila's mother collapsed on to the sofa at Deirdre's side. She was still fanning herself.

"Is there Irish in your family that you called your girl Sheila?" asked Deirdre, when the silence between them stretched out too long for comfort.

"No, what gave you that idea?"

"Sheila's an Irish name."

"Oo no, I just liked it."

So fat and stupid and pleased with herself, she was, that Deirdre longed to snub her. "Names should stand for something," she said. "Or mean something."

"It does. Sheila means a good sort!" yelled Sheila's stepfather. "Hey, Sheila, I reckon you're the best sort at the party, except for your old woman. If Hugh kicks you out, I'll take you on."

"You'll do no such thing," called the fat one, not too pleased with the idea.

Deirdre sat quiet and aloof, watching the hurly-burly. She looked down at her hands, folded in her lap, the left one with the gold band overlapping the other; on the right one she wore the gold ring, with two snakes entwined, their eyes still glittering. Her hands were pale on her pale silk dress, ashes of roses Reg called it; it was a present from him.

The room swam with smoke. Behind the grey haze the paper flowers from Mexico looked washed-out. Someone had stubbed out a cigarette on Sheila's bouquet of pink camellias, the same colour as her dress and hat. I suppose her nerve failed her, thought Deirdre, she didn't dare to put on white. She looked across to Sheila, doing a rumba or a mambo or a zulu or whatever she called it, with her shoes off.

Reg bent over to give his orders to Tim, who struck a chord and yelled them all down. "Righto, you peasants, that's enough. Come on, sample the fun of the fair. It's all waiting for you. It won't cost you a rahzoo. Let's go!"

Two by two they all swarmed after Tim, over the rolled-back carpet and the floor wet with beer. From the clothes-basket where he slept, Reg's red kelpie growled at them. Reg stopped to pat him and rub his ears.

"Come on Deirdre," he called to her. "Quick love, I can't wait. You'll have to catch me up. Got to get over there before these hooligans wreck the joint."

"You go, Reg, I'll be along in a minute."

They were pushing their way down the narrow stairs, the pack of them, old ones and young ones, noisy as a bus-load of kids out on a spree. The boy called Kevin bowed to her as he went out: he'd be the one from the Christian Brothers that played Romeo in the balcony scene, when they tried to con Hugh into Juliet, but he kept on forgetting his lines, accidentally on purpose, and someone else had to do it. Or so Reggie said, full of stories about his boy, Hughie this, Hughie that, my boy Hughie, till you'd had as much as you could stand. Still, he's a nice-looking boy, not too far short of what Reggie claims for him, which is surprising, considering what a loudmouth he can be, that Reggie. He's lucky, though. It must be a gift, not to have your past sealed up inside you, just be able to open your mouth and blab them out, all the wrongs done to you and all the messes you've made. Easy to get rid of them that way.

Deirdre watched the last of them go. At the top of the stairs the fatso stumbled, with her high heels caught in Tiger's trouser cuff.

"Whoops-a-daisy," called someone. "Don't do that or you'll break your neck."

Deirdre crossed to the balcony, and stood looking out across the cove, then to the street below. There they were, scooting across, dodging cars, squealing, making for the dark end of the pier. As she watched, the lights blazed out, so Reg had got there, or Timmy. The two last to leave the party, running late, almost got skittled by a taxi. The driver put his head out and swore at them.

Unwillingly she turned away from the window and went to make herself ready for the next hour that had to be got through. Someone had left the cistern running. She pulled the rusty chain twice, one hard pull then a soft one, the way you had to. She ran cold water into the basin over her wrists, splashed it then on her hot cheeks.

The one who faced her from the glass had a red stain over her cheekbones, and freckles faded pale after the long winter. With her wide-open dark eyes, her curly dark hair pulling loose from its combs, she looked like—

"I look like a witch," she said, under her breath.

She called goodbye to the hired help, glad that for once she wasn't stuck with the wettex cloth. Her feet clattered on the wooden stairs, the way they always did. Outside the air was cool, a light breeze lifting the papers in the gutter. Between the clouds, a few stars were sprinkled over a dark sky. No moon, though.

The fun of the fair, he'd called it, Tim. By now he had set everything going. The crowd that had nearly burst open the flat looked skimpy in the fun park, like a poor roll-up on a wet Saturday afternoon. The dodgems were doing good business, they always did; the merry-go-round wasn't short of riders, either. And the Ferris wheel, with nobody inside the cars, was going round and up to the moon that had just come out from behind the clouds.

Tim was shouting, top-note as usual. "I know why I got an invite. Sweated labour!" He was manning the merry-go-round.

"Come on Bob, get off the horsie and give us a hand!"

"No way!" Bob shouted back. "I'm off duty."

Hugh and Sheila rode side by side on two grey horses with hardly any hairs left in their tails. That was one of Reggie's whinges: the kids keep pulling the hairs out. Fast as I put the tails back they've got mangy manes, he kept grumbling. Let me catch one of them in the act, I'll warm his behind for him.—

The music-box inside the merry-go-round was grinding out Moonlight and Roses. Reg waved to her as he went circling past. He was standing on the platform next to Sheila's mother, who was straddling a horse, its head poking out of her orange skirts. The second time round Reg bowed first then beckoned her to come aboard.

No doubt about Reg, he had his own style. That old fellow, he could have done anything in life he wanted, she thought, if only he'd stuck at it. No sooner did he get something running right, though, than he was sick of it, crazy to get on to the next thing that caught his fancy. He never ran out of stories, never. He teased her because she had none to tell. How come you never talk about your past, eh? Still waters run deep, I reckon, Deirdre.

We're a funny pair, she thought now, as she had often thought before, it's a miracle we've lasted this long. I'm lucky that he loves me and he never goes snooping, and, yes, I like him well enough. For all his tales of the past, he lives in the present, and that's balm to me. So I'll let it go on and see what comes of it. And sooner or later I'll be given a sign, go or stay, the way I was before.

Deirdre stood, thinking her thoughts, by the waxworks. The Palace of Waxworks it said over the arched doorway. The door was open; Reg must have used his own key. A lot of the time they didn't bother to open up, she couldn't be spared from the kiosk or ticket-box just to take the kids around. Reg didn't care. Open when you like, love, and close when you feel inclined. You're the queen of the show. Deirdre waited, her bare arms suddenly goosefleshed by the night air, cold, with the last skerrick of winter still in it. She felt a long distance from that crowd on the hurdy-gurdy there, and the other pack, poking balls into the clowns' mouths.

"Let's have a go on the Ferris wheel," called the boy with a great big nose and a face covered with pimples.

How did he get into the party, Deirdre wondered. One of Sheila's mob, maybe, her cousin or something.

"Come on. Auntie Midge," he was yelling. That elephant, she was called Midge, so it seemed. A joke, maybe, short for midget.

"I'm taking this chick." Reggie had Sheila by the arm. "Go and grab Deirdre, Hugh. Pick her up and carry her if she gives any lip." Deirdre moved into the dark entrance. From the shooting-gallery a rifle cracked. She tensed, then relaxed. Behind her stood Hugh.

"Come and have a ride on the Ferris wheel?" It was Hugh's voice, but it might almost have been Reggie's, ocker as they called it, but deep and pleasant for all that.

"No," she answered. "I hate it. It makes my head spin."

"Alright," he said, after a moment. "How about taking me round the waxworks then?"

Deirdre hesitated. She didn't like to have them sneered at, not that it mattered much, and no doubt they were a mouldy collection. Still, you like what you like, and something about them soothed her: anyway she didn't want them made fun of. Little kids, they were alright, it didn't take anything much to please them. She liked opening up once in a while to take the kids on a guided tour.

She glanced up at him and made up her mind: he wouldn't be poking fun, he had the good manners the Brothers whacked into them, the boys they got hold of early enough. So she turned on the lights. The corridor lay in darkness, a pool of light around each wax figure. Where they came from nobody knew, not the fellow who'd leased the park to them when he got sick, nor any of his offsiders. They were just there, that's all. Maybe they'd come from two or three different places, some of them were in better shape than others. A few were taken from history and the rest were tortures, except for one, slipped in from nowhere.

Hugh gave a grunt of pleasure. "Gee I love waxworks," he said, smiling down at her. He went over to stand near the first one, the little prince in the tower, pleading with Hubert for his life. Or eyesight, the same thing. It was the one that always drew Deirdre closer, the one she always hurried past, just sneaking a look out of the corner of her eye to see if it was still there.

Now, first glancing, then gazing full, she beheld it as she had never done before: the little boy looking upwards, his lips parting, praying for mercy, next to him the young man, sideways on, his lips parted the same way. She caught her breath, taking the picture in.

He turned to her and the moment was over. His square white teeth caught the light as he spoke. "I know that one, anyway. Poor little kid. They were cruel old days, alright."

He moved on to the next circle of light and stood still, his hair bright as a new penny. "Bluebeard," he murmured. "Gee, pretty grisly, isn't it? Do the kids like it?"

"The boys do. The little girls squeal. I don't think they're frightened if someone's holding on to their hands."

He nodded and crossed to the next one, down the end of the corridor. It was Cleopatra, holding the snake to her breast.

"Pretty quick way to go, they tell me."

He turned the corner and she followed. He liked this one: that woman sitting by the guillotine, knitting. The guillotine didn't work when he tried it.

"What happened?" he asked. "There's a part missing."

"Some kid souvenired it. They're little devils, some of them, all they do is wait till your back's turned."

He was shaking his head, smiling but serious. "Hope I don't get any like that in my squad. Darned if I'd know how to handle them."

"Went by the rules, did you? When you were a kid?" He wasn't much more than a kid now.

"'Fraid so. I never wanted to step out of line."

Round the back of the U-turn he went, past the fellow stretched out on the rock for the eagles to peck at, not stopping to give him more than a glance. And the hunchback, he didn't linger over that one, either.

Now he was standing in front of the last one, if you could call it any part of the show. It was a box where a headless woman lay, all wax, in a long dress draped in folds. On her breast her hands were folded, one over the other, beautiful long fingers she had. Every picture tells a story, thought Deirdre, and those hands, they look as if she's glad to be done with it all, what life handed out to her.

"Who's this?" He leaned over the box, as full of life as the woman inside was short of it. He put out his hand and all but touched the wax hands. She rested her eyes on him, Reggie's boy Hugh, filled with pleasure at the thought of a lad whistling about the place. It'll rub off on both of us, his father and me, she thought. There's nothing as lovely as a young one with all life opening up to him.

"Do you know who it is?" he asked again.

She shrugged. "Nobody knows anything about her."

"What happened to her head?"

She turned up her palms. "It's a mystery. I guess there's a story behind it, if only we knew. Maybe she's better off without her head."

She turned to go. He hesitated, then followed.

"Yeah, maybe," he said. The three years in America had given his voice a bit of a twang.

Deirdre Kincaid laughed aloud. "You'll bring new life into the old place. We were needing another young one," she told him. "When do you start your coaching?" She went ahead of him to the door, then turned to catch his answer.

"Oh, not till the pool opens in October. About five weeks from now, I guess. We'll be away for a month or so, till our money runs out. But Sheila's going to work too, so we'll soon get on our feet. She's going to teach the tiddlers to swim."

Deirdre switched out the lights. Her voice, in the dark, sounded spooky to her ears. "And will you be teaching the wobbegongs, then?"

They came out of the dark into a place all shattering noise, dodgems grinding and people screeching. She looked up into his face and saw that he was not yet back from the world they'd just left.

"Wobbegongs?" he asked uncertainly. "Oh, sharks!" He threw back his head and laughed. "No. I'll be doing the senior squads. The serious swimmers." He moved away from her.

"What would they be, serious swimmers?" she called after him, but he didn't hear. She watched while he swung up on to the merry-go-round, now gathering speed, while he flung his leg over the horse, sitting very straight, there next to his bride, his long legs almost touching the ground, his bright head moving away from her, while the broken-down music-box kept wheezing on.

2

Her back was beginning to ache, so she gave up scrubbing for a moment, and let her eyes rest on the seagulls, wheeling low to the water. When I was a girl, she mused, seasons went by weather and by feasts and by Saints' days. Now they go by how much donkey-work there is to be done, you can't draw a breath through summer and you put in time all winter long. Spring, you've got to get rid of last summer's dirt that you closed the door on at Easter: by then you'd had a bellyful of it, if you'd had to clean it up at summer's end you'd take a hatchet to the whole concern. Maybe I won't be here by next spring. Maybe Reg'll want to let the lease go by then, and be thinking of running a lion park or whatever comes into his head, and he'll rope me in to give the cubs their milk from a titty-bottle. Or maybe I'll go back on the boats again. But I'd miss him and that's the truth, you get used to company and he's kept his end of the bargain well—not that he had much choice—and I've grown accustomed to his face, as they say in the song.

She looked at Reg, done up in a boiler-suit long past its prime, dipping a towel into a bucket of suds and squeezing it out, so he could wash the clowns' faces. Might save him a job of painting, so he'd said. Plenty of patience he had when he needed it, that was the—(she counted)—thirteenth face he'd washed this morning, every one of them the dead spit of the one before.

"They could do with a touch-up, Deirdre," he said, following her eyes. "A bit of red at the end of their noses, it'd do wonders for the look of them. I'll be glad of a schooner when I'm through, it's a cow of a job. What d'you reckon, Dee, a nice blob of scarlet, think it'd be worth a try?"

"Nothing'd fix their stupid mugs up," she answered. "You don't know how I hate them, they're bad enough when they keep still, but when they start wagging their heads I could throttle them."

"Don't do that." He wiped the fourteenth face tenderly and gave it a scratch behind the ear, "They bring us in a lot of loot, don't you boys? You think about it, Dee, they're one of our biggest money-makers when you work it all out. Don't cost much to run and they never go wrong, hardly. Touch wood."

"There's nothing in them to go wrong."

"Still—Don't you go biting the hand that feeds you. You have a think how many times you see me and Tim crawling on our bellies under the hurdy-gurdy." Reg sighed. "It's seen better days. Like the old bloke that runs it."

Deirdre went back to scrubbing the kiosk counter. The shelves were drying; they smelled like eucalyptus, this new lot of disinfectant was a lot stronger than the last, lathered up better, too. Harder on your hands, though: everything's got a price. Two of the nails she'd grown long in winter were broken, and another hanging by a shred, she'd have to start clipping them short again. Not that she cared much, she was long past all that fooling about with her looks. All those years on the boats, she'd kept them cut short. Funny that, when she was a girl she did nothing but spruce herself up, nearly went mad when she got a pimple, even. Nails, toenails, not an inch of her body escaped her eyes. Stupid, you are, coming into your teens, she thought, mooning about your looks as if they're a lucky charm. There's no lucky charm anywhere. She went savagely back to her scrubbing. All there is, it's whatever deal you get handed out to you, like it or lump it, it's all you're getting. Then after a while you learn to look after yourself, so nothing'll ever get to you again.

"I reckon you're the only girl in Australia who still uses sandsoap," called Reggie, cocking his eye at her. He was always ready to be sociable, nothing he loved better than the sound of his own voice.

"I'm no girl," she said shortly, not in the mood for chit-chat. "But I'm a good work-horse, if that's what you're wanting."

"Never crossed my mind, Deirdre, love." He put his towel

over the clown's face and gave her all his attention. "The day I walked into the fish and chips and saw you I said to myself that's the girl for me. Talk about luck! You take on a job for a couple of weeks to oblige a cobber and you end up with a nugget of gold. When I looked at you dipping the fish in the batter, with a bit of flour on your chin, your curls all standing on end—" He was grinning at her, that grin like a guttersnipe's that got her in, same as it got everyone in. He didn't even know he had it, let alone how it warmed everyone up.—"Your overall covered in grease, giving the kids two bob's worth for five cents—I tell you what, love, if they'd run a poll for queen of the fish shops you'd have walked it in."

"I mightn't have had too much competition," said Deirdre, biting back a laugh. Reg had a funny way of pulling your leg and meaning what he said, at one and the same time.

"Less than the dust beneath thy chariot wheels," he was singing, moving the towel back and forth over the last of the stupid faces. Then he threw the towel down, swinging round, all ears, when he heard a voice hail him, Hugh's voice, and there was Hugh, bounding in from the entrance.

Deirdre put down her brush, watching the two of them, full of smiles, both of them, to be meeting. Reg was hugging the boy, all but kissing him.

"Where's Sheila? Where's the little beauty? Did they steal her away from you up Surfers?"

"No, she's just home unpacking. We got hold of a nice little flat just over from the pool, well, tell you the truth it's not so hot, but it's nice and handy. If you've got to get going at five, you've got to live right on the job."

Deirdre stood smiling, waiting for Hugh to turn to her. At last he did.

"How's tricks, Deir- Deirdre?" he greeted her, stumbling over her name. "Sorry I didn't notice you there. Sprucing things up a bit, are you?"

"That'll be the eighth wonder of the world, the day this place looks spruce.—But you do. You went away gold and you came back—" She stopped short when she saw him flush, embarrassed by her praise. Reggie, now, he couldn't get enough of it. Some like it, some don't. "Enjoy your holiday, did you?"

"Gosh yes, Sydney seems tame after it. We had great weather. You ought to see Sheila if you think I'm brown." When Deirdre didn't answer he went on. "Speaking of Sheila, she sent you these. Dad, this one's for you."

As usual Reg couldn't wait to get his hands on it. If no one gave him presents he went out and bought them for himself. He nearly dropped it in his hurry to get the paper off.

"Oops, look out! It's breakable," Hugh put in quickly. "She thought it'd give you a laugh."

The wrappings fell to the concrete. Reg held his present in both paws, a pottery figure of a fellow in a country dunny, with his back turned.

"I don't think you'd better make it go," said Hugh doubtfully, shifting from one foot to the other.

But Reg was pressing every little nook and cranny he could find, until at last he hit on the right place. The door swung open and the fellow turned round, a terrible simpleton with his hands on his fly, aiming fair and square at Reg and spraying his face.

Roaring with laughter, Reg wiped his face dry. "Nifty, eh? Wonder who thought that up?—Now, Deirdre, don't frown like that, you're a woman of the world, love."

Hugh was holding out a parcel to Deirdre. In his bright blue T-shirt and shorts, with his brown skin and his hair bleached gold by the sun, he looked like a travel-poster: Come to Sunny Australia. Slowly she broke the sealing tape and folded the paper back. There were two tea-towels, one printed with half-naked girls, the other with scenes of Surfers Paradise.

"Who chose them?" asked Deirdre, turning them over, then looking away at the black grit in the water lapping the pier.

"Sheila did. That's her department." He glanced back to Reg, who was acting as if he was in seventh heaven, making the simpleton go back and forth at top speed.

"What made her think I was short of dish clouts?"

"Oh!" Hugh was taken aback. "She thought you might like a souvenir of Surfers."

"It's a place I've never seen fit to go to." Deirdre spoke coldly. Then she looked at the boy's uneasy face and she felt ashamed that she'd needled him. He's only a kid, she thought. She smiled at him, first with her eyes, then with her lips, the way she'd learned in the old days. "But thank her for the thought anyway, that's what counts."

"Gosh it's a great place they've got up there. Talk about go-ahead. I nearly thought I was back in the States."

Reggie stopped playing with his toy and scowled. "Now then Hughie, none of that talk. Australia's good enough for anyone. The greatest little country in the world, bar none. Don't you rubbish your own country, boy."

"I didn't, dad. All I said was— Well when I think what one of the big promoters would do with a place like this, right on the water— Gee, how often do you get a pretty little bay like this only a stone's throw from the ocean? Think of the money you could make if you wanted to build it up."

"What do I use for capital, tell me that? And one thing you're forgetting, it's only leased out." Reggie was red as a lobster.

"You could borrow. In the States they're not frightened of credit. They use advertising—I bet you never advertise. That's what my course was all about, using the media to—"

Reg had had enough of him. "Let me tell you something boy, you start doing that and you'll end up in the shit—sorry, Dee, but that's what I meant anyway. All that malarky you're talking, that's what's making the country go to the dogs. The rides are there for the kids when they get off the ferry, if they feel like it. If they don't want to come, I'm the last one to want to con them into it." He thought of something to clinch it. "Anyway what sort of bank's going to hand it over to an old bugger like me. You wake up to yourself, boy."

Hugh was shuffling about, he had on new sandals, bought fresh for his honeymoon, no doubt. "Keep your shirt on, dad. It was just a suggestion, that's all. But you've got to admit it's not the most up-to-date fun park in the world."

"If they want something flash they can go to the place down the road." Reggie was calm again, that's if you could ever call him calm. "Kids don't know the difference. Long as they've got a bellyful of lemonade and some machine to shake Jesus Christ out of them, they're happy as Larry." He turned gloomy. "I've got problems though. The place is alive with rats. I don't know where to start getting rid of them."

"There's some new stuff they're using in the pools in the States," said Hugh, eager to please. "It's great stuff. Tasteless, odourless. Works like magic. Great stuff!"

"The rats mightn't think so," said Deirdre, rolling out the paper to line the shelves.

"What's a man to do? I don't like the job any more than you do, Deirdre, but you have a think about it, you'll see how I'm placed. A rat can have a thousand babies a year." He had got himself into a bad temper and now he was casting round for something else to whinge about. Hugh had started it, slinging off at the park: he had a thin skin, Reggie, for all he was such a blowhard.

What about that, she thought in amusement: blowhard, it's a word I never even heard before Reg said it. I'm even getting to think like him. No doubt about Reggie, he leaves his mark on you.

He was wound up now, anything'd do to whinge about.

"The merry-go-round's had it, there's no two ways about it. The motor's packed up, or close on. Wish I could get hold of a classy job, it's the merry-go-round that makes or breaks a fun park. If we have a good season I might shout myself one."

"Dooley mightn't let you put it in," Hugh reminded him.

"To hell with Dooley!" snapped Reg. "He's leased it out to me. A hundred bloody Dooleys won't stop me till the lease runs out. That's what I really need, the best merry-go-round in Australia, then all our troubles'd be over. Wish I had the dough."

"If wishes were horses then beggars could ride," murmured Deirdre. He'd never be done dreaming, that's what kept him going.

He turned to her then, and slapped her on the behind, sham-sexy. "That'll be enough back-chat from you."

Hugh yawned, showing all his back teeth, not a filling in any of them. "Sorry," he said, putting his hand over his mouth. "Gosh I'm sleepy."

"It's called honeymoon hangover," Reg told him. "Think nothing of it."

Hugh didn't bite. "Better see I get my sleep from now on. If I don't keep early hours I'll never last the distance. Like the old days, eh dad?"

Reggie stopped what he was doing and stood there half-smiling, a pot of glue in one hand and a horse's tail in the other. "Great time, wasn't it? Not too many blokes have the luck to teach their boy to swim, then see him State champion first, then Australian-"

Now Deirdre yawned; it was a story she'd heard many times over. So had Hugh.

"Got to run, dad," he put in, when Reggie paused for breath. "I've got to see Mr Peters down at the pool."

"Don't let him put it over you, boy," Reg called after him. "You might reckon he's a good guy, but these pool managers, they can't help flogging the willing horse. They've seen me with my tongue hanging out for a rest, and all they do is fill up the lanes till the kids are squashed like sardines in a tin, then leave it to the poor bloody coach to sort it out. Don't tell me about pool managers. You start as you mean to end."

Hugh, who had halted to listen, got going again. "Righto. See you, dad. See you, Deirdre."

Reg pushed the tail into the hole and fixed it with glue.

"Looks a bit skimpy," he judged, standing back. "Never mind, we'll just have to make a little go a long way, as the monkey said when he peed over the gap."

Deirdre heard his voice, without taking it in. She was watching the boy go, his long legs and his quick step. The place seemed empty without him. Something in the way they move, the young ones, their sweet breath and a sort of dew on their skin. Not much in their heads, though. All at once she remembered she had a bone to pick with Reg.

"Listen Reg, you cut that out, acting sexy. Why've you got to make out you're Casanova? That's why I took you on, so I could get away from the maulers. I told you that. You've got no heart for smoodging, any more than I have. So stop kidding you've just had a testicle transplant or I'll up and leave." She picked up the scissors and began to hack at the shelf-paper, ignoring his injured face.

He got ready to spruik, but the merry-go-round beat him to it. All by itself it started turning, singing one of its wheezy songs. Did your mother come from Ireland, it was singing.—Maybe there was a kid inside, monkeying about with the works.

With a curse Reggie jumped up on the platform and down the other side, making for the motor tucked away there behind the painted panels and mirrors.

3

The flat was mouldy with age, so nothing could ever make it look halfway decent. You could get rid of the cockroaches, but they were back in a couple of weeks. Back there in Belfast, where her aunt lived, down the area stairs, it had the same cracked paint peeling off, the same smell of damp, along with another funny sort of musty smell, it took a hundred years of people's dirt to get a stink like that. So I came to the other side of the world to have it greet me, she reflected. Rusty didn't help, either, he was getting the smell of an old dog, and he left his hairs wherever he lay down, on the end of Reggie's bed, everywhere round. The last boat she worked on, it was starting to get that look; the top brass were talking about getting it refurbished or broken up. So Dora said, anyway. Wonder what happened to Dora? Keep in touch, sweetie, that was the last thing Dora said. Though Deirdre had nodded, she had no such intention: put things behind you and you're better off.

Funny though, I feel comfortable here, Deirdre thought. It's got enough cupboards to keep my stuff in, and a stove to rustle up a bit of a meal, and if it was brand-new I wouldn't know what to do with myself. The truth is, I'm not much of a housekeeper, I never was. Auntie Nora, she kept the place like a pig-sty, and my mother, she wasn't much better, what I remember of her. Twenty seven years since she died, thirty four she was, maybe thirty five, same age as me. She shivered: a goose going over my grave, she thought. Wonder what she felt before she jumped. Funny, she had no need to take it that way, she could have got rid of the baby when the fellow dumped her, or come to that she could have had it and be damned to the lot of them. No she couldn't, the priests would have torn her apart, down in Kerry there you couldn't step out of line. Deirdre shut her mind: waste of time, thinking.

She gave Rusty his weet-bix, he wasn't too keen on them, but he wagged his tail and got out of the basket, sniffing at the bowl and turning his nose up before he decided there was nothing better offering. He was Reggie's fourth red kelpie. Reg reckoned he'd have six before he kicked the bucket. And the last one, he said, they'd die at the same moment and be buried in the same grave, so neither one'd be left lamenting. He talked a lot of hot air, Reggie did. No doubt about it, the dog loved him, anyone else was just a fill-in while he waited for Reggie to come back. He'd made no bones about showing her she was second-best, not that she cared, the less ties you had the easier it was to move on.

She went back to the stove. Reg was in the shower, warbling away. He never shut up. I get a reprieve from him at night, though. I bet he's in there talking in his sleep or snoring all night long. When she shut her door at night she was ready for some quiet. When she worked really hard she couldn't get enough sleep, she hardly had time to put her head on the pillow before it was morning.

"Your bacon and egg's cooked, Reg," she called.

"Coming, love. What sort of a day is it?"

She put her plate down on the plastic tablecloth and went to the balcony to stare out across the bay towards Sydney. Today it was dark blue, no yachts out yet, no glitter but a lot of little choppy waves. The pine trees down by the water had long shadows, the sunlight was pale on the pale fringe of sand. All the shops along the pier were closed, no one about at all.

"Windy," she told him.

"The sun out?"

"Yes. No heat in it, though."

"Long as the sun keeps shining they'll straggle in. Long weekends they've got time to fill in."

Now he was out, his face rosy from the shower, his skin bleeding in two places where he'd scraped it raw. There was a tuft of hair he'd missed. A strong smell of shaving-lotion followed him out of the bathroom. He was done up in a pair of new jeans and a dark blue skivvy. No doubt he looked a Guy

Fawkes. Rusty had his doubts too and came over to sniff at him.

"Don't think too much of your old man's new image, by the look of you," he said, pulling his dog's ears.

"Who would?" she said, briefly. "Do you want tea or coffee? What made you get yourself done up like a sore toe?"

He looked down at his jeans, not too sure that he liked them after all. "Young Hugh. It was his fault. He says there's nothing like them for comfort. Reckon I look a galah, Deirdre? I've got a bit of a beer-gut. Maybe it wasn't such a good idea." He stood there crestfallen, looking down at his new pants, stiff as boards.

"No, you look good," she lied. As well as making him look a galah, they'd be a menace to wash. "Sit down, your breakfast won't be worth eating."

Still he dilly-dallied. "Did the boys come for the keys?"

"Tim did. Bob's still in bed."

"That bloody Bob, he needs a rocket shoved up his bum and set light to." She turned her back. The kettle was boiling. "Well I'll tell you why I've got no appetite, Dee, it's these piles, they crucify me. I'd just as soon be nailed to the cross as put up with them sometimes."

"Don't talk like that. It's blasphemy."

"I thought you'd had a bellyful of the church."

"I have. But there's no need to talk like that. Besides—"

"Besides what?" He was sitting down; whatever he said, he loved his tucker.

"Besides, someone might hear and then you'd get paid back."

Reg moaned and shifted in his chair to show what pain he was in. "Alright, Dee, but you don't know what I'm suffering."

"You don't eat enough vegetables, that's half your trouble."

"That helps, does it? Alright, you cook me up a potful and I'll get 'em down if it kills me."

Deirdre was stacking up the breakfast dishes, running water in the frying-pan. They could wait till she came back. "Now don't you go bringing home a case of cabbages. I'll get a bunch of spinach and some lettuce. And prunes, they're good too. Hurry up, Reg, we've got a big day ahead of us."

"Hope so. But I tell you this, if I'm not better by Easter I'll let the quacks have a go at me. They fixed Jacky up. One week of hell he had after they sliced him open and after that he never had a twinge. That's what he reckons, anyway."

Deirdre took off her apron and picked up a cardigan. "I'll see if I can cure you first. From now on you can have orange juice to start the day."

"Gawd Struth," he said, filling his mouth too full, as usual, spilling egg down his new skivvy. "All of a sudden I'm tied up to Florence Nightingale."

"There's your tea in the pot. I'll be going," she said, over her shoulder. "You coming, Rusty?" Rusty looked from one to the other of them and made his choice. He flopped down at Reg's feet.

At the fun park things were just starting to hum. The ferry that pulled in was crammed with families out for the day. Most of them headed straight for the beach, but there were plenty left for the big amusement pier, as it was called, down the road, and a good-sized dribble for Reg's Fun Park, as their new sign said outside. Some of the trippers were still in their winter clothes, but the majority had got out in their spring duds, with a cardigan over the top. They'd be sorry: there was a bite in the air. The young mothers were plastered with make-up, every year they had more stuff around their eyes. Even at nine in the morning they had their war-paint on, maybe though it was just yesterday's not washed off.

The two poodles that belonged to the chemist over the road trotted in and squatted down, side by side, in front of the dodgems.

"Get home, you bastards!" roared Reggie, from the Ferris wheel. Too late. "Clean it up, Dee love, I can't leave here."

So she did: there was nobody else to do it. It was going to be one of those days.

In the lavatory, where she went to wash her hands, she almost tripped over a broken lemonade bottle. They were on the job early today. She cleaned that up, too. Someone had been writing on the wall: Troy Rigson sucks dogs balls this is true. Someone else on the early shift: it hadn't been there last night. She washed her hands with the square of white soap that smelled cool and sweet, relishing the feeling of being clean before she moved on to the next dirty job.

She couldn't be in two places at once, Tim would have to do the tickets. She slipped behind the counter of the kiosk, where the kids were lined up, rapping their twenty cent pieces on the wood to hurry her up. They wanted lolly bananas, milk bottles, red Indians, jelly-beans and freckles, as many of them as you could get for twenty cents, crammed into a paper bag. Their mothers caught her eye and laughed, but the fathers didn't look too happy about the set-up. Poor cows, thought Deirdre, the women drive a hard bargain once they've got the men in their clutches. Tim was nowhere to be seen, so she left the kiosk to take over the ticket-box. A few of the blokes tried to give her the eye, they're hard-up, bored stiff with the wives they'd got. That's men, though. The seagulls started squawking as soon as the merry-go-round let up, sometimes she thought she'd go crazy if she heard just one more squawk out of them. The ferry-bell was ringing. The kids were belting hell out of the dodgems.

A fellow about forty shoved his kids on board the merry-go-round and leaned against the wall, trying to catch her eye. She ignored him, but he kept on trying. Some fellows, they're like that, they've got the roving eye and that's all there is to it, any woman'll do as long as it's not the one that's got them in tow. Reg would have been like that before the accident. After a while he gave up, collected his little girls and took off. Divorced, maybe, and this was his day for having charge of them. Pretty kids, both done up to kill, frills on the ends of their socks, even. Give me the boys though, any old day, she said to herself.

Bob had rolled out of bed at last. His little green eyes were still sleepy, he hadn't even washed the sleep out of the corners of them.

"You go, Deirdre," he said. "I'll take over the tickets."

A lazy coot he was, always after the easy jobs. This time she wasn't going to let him get away with it.

"I think Reggie wants you over at the Ferris wheel."

"I might do the clowns," he said. "Or the rifles."

That's all they needed, the rifles to get going. I hate the sound of rifles, she thought, I've had enough of that to last me all my life.

Two teenagers, dressed the same way, in jeans and T-shirts, one marked His and the other marked Hers, came up to complain. "We put our money in the machine and it didn't work."

"Try giving it a smack," she suggested.

"We did, but it didn't make any difference."

Deirdre left the box, with a quick glance across to the kiosk to see if anyone was waiting to be served. She took the cash-box with her, just in case. On her way to the machines she picked up half a dozen papers. A skinny kid was just getting ready to throw an empty bag down.

"Go on, love," she coaxed. "There's a bin over there. Set a good example, will you?"

He started to pull a face, but when she winked at him he thought better of it. "Go on, you," he ordered his little brother. "Shove it in the bin or I'll punch your face in."

"You and who else?" said his brother, shaping up, at the same time doing as he was told.

It was the second machine of the six that was stuck. Deirdre gave it half a dozen smacks on the back, but nothing happened. So she wrapped her arms right round it, and with a great effort managed to jiggle it back and forth. Then she pushed the lever in and snapped it back. Three cards flew out.

"Wow!" cried the girl. "We got a bonus."

Deirdre picked up the cards from the ground where they'd fallen and handed two of them over.

The boy read his first. "You will find fame and fortune in another land. Follow your star," he read, with an effort. Then he muttered, "Bullshit."

The girl was quicker and she did her best to put a bit of expression into it. "You will find fame and fortune in another land. Follow your star." She took hold of the boy's arm. "Looks like we're going the same place, Mark." She was keener on him than he was on her.

Thank God I'm done with all that, thought Deirdre. Better be an old man's darling than a young man's slave. She looked down at her card and read it.

"You will find fame—" She began to laugh. "It's always in another land, you notice." The girl laughed back.

The boy stayed sulky. "Come on, I want a go on the dodgems." He took off, the girl at his heels.

Deirdre gazed after them, both with long hair, his dirty, hers clean; both of them narrow in the hips. By the time I was her age I had all the hips and chest I was going to get. She sighed and pulled herself back to the present. Better get back on the job, no one else was likely to do it for her. No, there was Tim, behind the counter.

"Hey Deirdre," called Reg, when he saw her coming. "The fairy-floss machine's stuck. Go and fix it, will you love? You've got the knack of it."

She made her way through the thickening crowd, to the next job waiting for her.

4

Weekends were always busy now. They'd stay like that till summer's end, except for the odd time when the heavens opened and they were left stranded there, the three of them, Reg and Rusty nearly howling with misery, until at last he gave it best and shut up shop. There's no place on earth as miserable as a fun park on a pouring-wet Saturday afternoon. With a bit of luck it wouldn't happen too often, this season.

Weekdays it was different. The boys didn't come in, they had other jobs to go to, but Deirdre and Reg kept the place open every fine afternoon. Sometimes they did good business, sometimes bad, but it didn't matter much, there was no labour to pay and they never started the machines unless they had enough takers. Except for the clowns; for some reason Reg liked to set their silly heads wagging. Nothing to stay home for, really, you'd get the grues in the flat all by yourself, might as well be over here. And now with Thursday night shopping they'd get a bit of the overflow.

Every afternoon, regular as clockwork, right on two o'clock Hugh bounced in to make himself a milk shake, looking at his watch to check the time.

"Why don't you have a clock, Deirdre?" he asked.

"What for? Time goes the same way whether or not you check up on it."

He always made himself the same kind, always chocolate. He used a double serve of syrup and a double scoop of ice-cream. His eyes glistened as he took the first long pull on his straw. He didn't talk until he came to the very end of it, when he tipped the beaker up and slurped the last drop down. That done, it was time for him to go and see if his father wanted a hand. Reggie said he was a wizard with the dodgems, and since something needed to be done with them every second day, he more than earned his milk shakes. Those bloody kids, Reg always moaned, they do their best to turn the machines back into scrap-metal.

Hugh was happy in his job. He'd started work after the holiday weekend in October; at first it was murder, with him a new chum and the kids gasping for breath in the cold water. By now, he reckoned they were all getting the hang of it. He was browner than ever. Once in a while he'd lean against the counter and chat to Deirdre, the days that business was slack and Reg had no job lined up for him.

"Might as well have another milk shake," he said this day. "I've got three hard hours of coaching to put in when I get back. Soon as the days start to stretch out it'll be even more. Gosh I get thirsty."

Deirdre, tidying up the boxes of musk-sticks and jelly-beans, turned to look him over. She hadn't seen much of him since he'd started his coaching.

"You'd better look out for your dadda," she warned him. "He says you're drinking up all the profits."

"The lousy old buzzard," said Hugh affectionately, putting a third spoonful of syrup in the beaker. "Well look, Deirdre, it's like this, I'm only allowed two drinks of orange juice a day down at the pool. Not much for a growing boy, you've got to admit."

"Oh I reckon you've done your growing." She sized him up, six feet and more of him, covered from neck to ankle in the green and gold tracksuit he'd worn for his country abroad. "Is that your Olympic outfit?"

He looked suddenly shy, the way he had: it always reminded her he was only half grown-up.

"Yeah, the kids in the squad conned me into wearing it. Well, it's hard enough to get them to get stuck into their programme, so I— Looks as if I've got a big head, does it? They kept on and on till I gave in." He ducked his head and took a long gulp at the straw. "Thought I'd die of thirst."

"What makes you so thirsty?" She took her hand out of the freezer. She'd finished separating the ice-blocks from the paddle-pops, and her fingers were nearly frozen solid, too. She began to blow on them, trying to bring them back to life. "Just watching the kids swim up and down?" He was eyeing the broken jelly snakes she'd set aside to give to the kids short of a cent. "Like the look of those snakes, do you?" She rubbed her stiff hands together, to get movement back to them. "Here, hold out your hands." She dropped them into his outstretched palms.

"It's all good protein," he told her, eating them one by one. "We tell our swimmers to eat licorice or jelly-beans if they feel they've got to have something sweet. Apricot squares, they're nice too. Do you carry apricot squares?"

Deirdre started to laugh. "The trouble is they might never get sold, that's if I let you unpack them. Tell me what they're called, I'll order some."

"Apricot something—I'll find out the exact name for you. What did you ask me just then, Deirdre?" He frowned. "Oh yes, you asked if I just watched the kids swim up and down. You've got it all wrong. You're just taking the general view. It's very unenlightened."

"Unenlightened, is it?" she asked, for the pleasure of seeing him rise to the bait. "Now where did you pick that word up, Hugh?"

"We did it in our course. I majored in psychology, didn't dad tell you that? It comes into mass communication all the time. Let me put you in the picture, Deirdre." With each word he grew more serious, his face flushing with enthusiasm, even the tips of his ears going red, his eyes as blue as his father's, but clearer and younger. "A coach has got to be a psychologist, you know. As well as correcting strokes he's got to be able to psychoanalyze his swimmers. There's all those miles to be swum, or they won't make it to the top. Now some swimmers can take more stress than others, the girls are better on the whole—but some boys, they're sprinters, they're highly strung—"

"Which kind were you?" She leaned forward, chewing the end of a musk-stick.

"Oh—I was a stayer, I suppose—I wasn't anything much,

really."

"No," said Deirdre. "You weren't. Only world champion, that's all."

"Oh—dad did that. It was all his doing." When she shook her head he insisted on his point. "No, don't shake your head like that, it's the truth. He taught me all my strokes till I had them perfect. And he worked for hours on my starts and turns till they went like clockwork. See, you've got to swim hundreds of miles to take a second off your time, then you can throw it all away in the turns. That's how I won. I'd go into the turns behind, and I'd come out of them ahead. And he got me on to medley. See, I was too small for a freestyler—"

"You?" Deirdre looked at the height of him.

"I'm a dwarf. Backstrokers and freestylers, they need to be really tall these days. You think of a backstroker with his arms stretched out, they need to be about eight feet—"

"Eight feet," said Deirdre faintly. She'd never heard him wound up before. He'll give Reg a run for his money when he gets on his hobby-horse, she thought, putting the last of the musk-stick in her mouth. "Go on."

"Well I wasn't strong enough for a butterflyer, they need to be really compact. And there was Dave Lester, I could do a good 200 breaststroke, but not as good as his. So dad said what the hell, put it all together and see what sort of medley comes out. He wasn't coaching me by then, he was running a wedding photo business up in Brisbane. But he wrote to me every week and got down whenever he had the plane fare. He fixed up for me to board with Toby Beggs—"

"Who's he? I seem to have heard the name."

"You must have heard of Toby Beggs. Everyone has. The Olympic coach." He stared at her.

"Oh yes," she remembered. "He sent you a telegram." She began to laugh to herself, remembering Reg and the telegrams.

"You ought to laugh more often, Deirdre. It makes you look about thirty years younger."

"Then I'd be in my cradle!" she flashed back. "How old d'you think I am, a hundred? I'm nearly young enough to be Reg's daughter." She began to giggle, surprising herself. "That's if he started about fourteen, which no doubt he did."

Hugh was a bit of a prude, she'd noticed it before. He didn't crack a smile. "Oh—well—Did he ever tell you about the time he worked in a reptile park?"

"Thank God I didn't know him then!" cried Deirdre. "Else he'd have me milking the boa-constrictors."

Hugh was laughing too. "You don't milk them, do you? I don't think they're poisonous. They just crush you to death."

Deirdre shuddered. "I hate snakes."

"Then why do you wear that ring?" He pointed to her hand.

She was suddenly sombre. "Oh, that?—Somebody gave it to me," she added after a moment. She put her hands under the counter. "What made your father give up coaching? He never told me."

A shutter came down on that open face. "Oh, nothing much. Just had enough of it, I suppose. He's like that. He got into a bit of strife that landed him in hospital. When he came out he thought he'd have a go at something else."

"Go on about your coaching," she prompted, seeing him prepare to move off in search of Reggie. It gave a lift to the day, just having him around. A sight for sore eyes, my boy Hughie, Reg always said, and this time he wasn't exaggerating. I've never seen anyone glow with health before, she thought, it's the simple truth, every bit of him shines.

"What was I saying? Well, there's a lot more to it than meets the eye. Tapering, it's a fine art. You can ruin a whole season's preparation if your taper's wrong." He stopped, then thought of something that wound him up again. "We've got to make a stand against the East Germans. They've got schools for swimmers now."

"Like schools of fish?" she murmured.

"What?—No, not really. They swim and exercise, they've got

to do a bit of study of course. But they practically live in the water."

"Like fish," she said again. They must have brainwashed him over there in America, the terrible rubbish he was talking. She asked him now what she really wanted to know, about his medals. "Tell me about winning your medals, Hugh."

"There's nothing to tell." He stood there with a square of blue sky behind him, shifting from one foot to the other, torn between his shyness and wanting to live it all again. "Just—I won the two medleys, that's all. Don't know how I did it. I was lucky, I guess. No, don't snake your head. They're getting faster every year. I mightn't even make a final now."

"You'd be faster too."

"No, I was just lucky, that's all. But when I got up there on the victory dais—well, it was a great feeling."

"What did you think of?"

"Mostly I concentrated on not breaking down and making a fool of myself." He gave a bit of a laugh. "You get pretty emotional. Then I thought of dad, how pleased he'd be out there watching, he'd put more into it than I had, really. And when the band played, well gee, it all came home to me, what it all meant. It was a great feeling."

Deirdre was alight. Her cheeks grew hot as she cried out to him. "Oh I wish I'd been there! If I had a son, that's what I'd want for him." To see him outstrip all the rest of the world and stand up there while the drums rolled—Oh lucky Reggie, how lucky can you be, she thought with envy, fancy seeing your dreams come true. It'd be worth all the pain of living to see it all come right like that, just for once.

"It was a great feeling alright," he said again. "I'll show you the photos if you like."

"A caramel milk shake, please," said a cranky voice. "That's if it's not too much trouble. This is the third time I've been back, trying to get a bit of service."

Deirdre swung round. She spoke haughtily. "The kiosk's closed. Try over the road."

I'm nobody's slave, she wanted to say. I've been too many years at the beck and call of the riff-raff. What suited me then mightn't suit me now. Maybe I'm ready to go back to living, not just holding myself ready. She pushed back the curls that the breeze off the water was blowing over her face. The combs weren't made that could hold her hair in place.

"Got to get going," said Hugh, clammed up, feeling silly that he'd talked so much.

"You're a pretty good talker when you get going," she said, in fun. "Nearly as good as your father.—Though Reg, he's different, what he doesn't know he'll make up. I've never known anyone so fond of the sound of his own voice."

"Oh dad, he'll talk the leg off an iron pot."

"Who said?" rumbled Reg, staggering up to them with a great box full of trinkets and rubbish, Rusty at his heels. He set it down on the counter, "How about hosing it down for me, Hughie, there's no one much about. Those poodles, they've been at it again, they've got their spot marked out. I'll have the hose trained on them next time they stroll over. Look at these Dee, ever see such a load of muck in your life? I'll get you to box them up for me, give them a bit of razzamatazz."

Hugh was fingering them. "What are they?"

"They're the prizes for the clowns. They'll go on the bottom shelf. The boxes are in the office Dee, pink for the girls and navy-blue for the boys. Fix them up for me, will you love? I get them wholesale, Hughie." He held up a shell necklet. "This one's not bad. The cockroaches go in the blue boxes."

"What can you do with a rubber cockroach?" Hugh pulled one out, black and pudgy, but lifelike enough.

"You'd be surprised. Put 'em in someone's beer. Give someone a fright—We'll clean up with these, you'll see, they only worked out about ten cents each. Not bad, when you think they pay twenty cents a go. I'll get Tim on the job, he's got a good strong voice. If he bellows out every player gets a prize we'll be turning 'em away."

"What about the top shelf? The crockery and the pressure cooker. You wouldn't want them to go off too many times."

Reggie got that sneaky gleam in his eye and the wrinkles around them got deeper. "Well Hughie, they never seem to get won. Don't know why. But the middle shelf, the china pigs and the dressing-table sets, they go off once in a while." His new jeans looked like something ready to be given to the Salvation Army, all wrinkled and greasy, with the back pocket torn. No doubt about Reg, it was a war to the death between him and whatever he put on. When he caught her looking he hitched his jeans up over his belly. "I got into a bit of strife with the truck this morning," he told her.

"Got to get going." Hugh turned away, moving abruptly. "I promised Shee I'd pick her up and take her shopping. They slapped another class on her yesterday."

"Gawd Struth, the luck of some blokes. They get hold of a doll like that and all they think about's getting her to work." Deirdre glanced up sharply. Reg got the message. "Just like I did," he said, going on without a break. "There's a lot of low cunning in the Kincaids, you've got to grant us that, Deirdre."

They smiled together, father and son, their lips turning up the same way. No doubt he's a nice kid, thought Deirdre, watching him when he loped off to pick up the hose as he'd been told. Pity he's hitched up to that little bitch, still, long as he keeps her away from here.

"Alright Reg, give me the box and I'll get started."

"Tonight'll do, while we're watching telly. There's no great rush." He hoisted the box on to his shoulder and made for the office.

Hugh, the hosing done, sped out to the rusty beat-up car he'd paid a hundred dollars for, and fixed up; with a rattle and a whoosh he was on his way.

5

It was blazing hot for November, too hot for comfort. Reg kept talking about Grafton, how he wanted to take her up to see the jacarandas, wherever you look it's purple, he kept saying, it's got to be seen to be believed. Just two pins, that's all he needed to close up and take her to see for herself.

"I'll take your word for it, Reg," she told him. "I'm well off where I am."

That's how she felt at the moment, well off. She liked the heat, she couldn't get enough of the sun. Working on the boats all those years she'd had to get used to a change of climate. You started off from England in winter and sailed into an Australian autumn, lovely it was, warmer than summer in Ireland: it always gave you a pleasant surprise. But the other way round, going from an Australian winter to an English autumn, that wasn't so good. Funny when you think about it, going from the top of the world to the bottom, and back again, year in, year out. If she had her pick she'd stay here for good, no place is ever perfect, and just to feel warm enough, there's a lot to be said for that. And the colour of the skies, that rich blue, and the look of the night sky, with all those stars. On the boat you got used to sea and sky, most of the time that's all there was to see. Except for the ports: the strangest feeling it gave you, walking in places where you'd never been before, and when next trip came they'd still be there, but if you dropped dead nobody'd know or care. For years she'd wanted it like that: no strings. It was only when she got measles and they stood her down for a trip, that broke up the pattern. She took the job in the fish shop on impulse, just for something to do till the boat came back.

And there was Reggie, popping up out of nowhere like a jack-in-the-box, giving her the big rush, refusing to take no for an answer, talking her into that day at the races.

"It's Jericho or bust! I've got every bean I own on that little filly. She looks like you, Deirdre. If she wins we'll paint the town red—"

It seemed like a sign. But for all that her heart fell to her boots when the horse flew in, and Reg jumped on his panama, then picked her up and swung her round.

So that was the prize, she thought, half sour, half muffling a giggle: hard labour for life. A wedding that was all sham whichever way you looked at it; no wonder we both kept it dark. I'll dress you in ermine, he'd promised her: wait a year or two, love, and I'll dress you in ermine.

Skunk, more like it, thought Deirdre. But all in all it was a good enough life, and he'd kept his promise, not that he had any choice. He was always full of schemes and promises. When she leaned out of the balcony to see the night sky, he was ready to take her to Ayers Rock—or what about Gundagai?—Armidale—Bathurst—

In the end she'd had to squash him. "No thanks Reg, I'm a city girl. The only year I spent in the country—" She stopped.

"What, Dee?"

"Nothing."

He didn't keep on, he knew when it was time to stop. "As long as you like it here love, that's all that worries me."

Well, she did like it here. She felt at home in this run-down seaside town, with the main streets so old, some of the shops with tiles missing and cracks in the brickwork, some of them in the back streets empty and boarded-up. She liked the sagging little houses, semi-detached or sometimes in terraces, propping each other up, with bits of cardboard behind broken window panes, and the steps with hollows in the middle from years of being walked on. Some of them had bits of garden in front with pansies or roses, but most of them just had a few marigolds growing in the long grass and maybe a cat sitting there. Like Belfast—no, it was worse there, no gardens at all, just the area stairs. When she went out to the country first she was lost with so much space around. The donkeys, they were nice, though.

Deirdre pulled herself up: it wasn't too often she let herself ramble on. She turned off the taps and picked up the long brush, and she forced herself into the job she hated most, scrubbing out the lavatories. Funny thing to end up doing, cleaning up other people's filth. On the boat, too. Lady This, Lady That, you couldn't believe the dirty habits of some of them till you saw it with your own eyes. They'd step out of the shower reeking of Chanel number 5 or 500, leaving their used pads on the ground to be picked up. She'd stood her ground. No, Lady Sweetacre—what a name, Lady Sweetacre—that's a personal matter. Report me to the captain, if you like, but he'll back me up when he hears what's at the bottom of it. I won.

Funny that about women, she had it in for me because her husband gave me the glad eye. She was welcome to him. If I'd wanted a bedmate it wouldn't have been him, with a face like an old mummy, and the whisky running out of his pores. Last thing in the world I wanted, look what it did to my mother, put her out of the frying-pan into the fire. One broke her heart and the other one left her in the lurch. You put yourself in their power and you're asking for trouble. One way or another they'll break your heart, that's the way they operate.

She flushed the last lavatory and left the brush soaking in a bucket of disinfectant. Wonder what's eating me today, I've spent more time thinking than I have in years. Queer that was about the boat, going backwards and forwards, year in, year out, hardly getting off even when I had the chance. Eating what was served up to me, doing the jobs lined up for me. Reg, he'd have died. Sometimes she wondered if he'd really held down all the jobs he'd reckoned. You take that one at the artificial eye makers, you wouldn't think there'd be much demand for them, but Reg said no, they did a roaring trade. His own eyes twinkled when he said it. Every now and then he'd hiss in her ear, see that bloke over there, his left eye's glass. He wasn't dull, you had to say that for him.

I'd better stop dreaming, I don't know what's got into me

today. She finished washing her hands and came out into the bright sunshine, blinking. The sun was high overhead; she'd taken advantage of a lull in trade to do the job she'd put off last night, she'd been too tired to force herself on. What day was it?—Friday? Yes, Friday. Except for the weekends, she lost track of the days.

She was vexed to see Sheila making the rounds of the place, the sun shining on her dyed blonde hair. Why would anyone have brown eyes and that oily brown skin and blonde hair on top of it. She'd better take care, it's coarse stuff, she'll grow a moustache when she gets around forty, I've seen it happen before this. Reg was trotting around next to her as if she was visiting royalty. She was done up to kill in a raspberry-coloured jacket over a white bikini, that showed her brown belly and ugly navel. First time I set eyes on her I had her measure, thought Deirdre. He's a mile too good for her, Hughie. Funny, some mothers they've got to stand by and see some little trollop like that get hold of their boys. Nothing they can do but grin and bear it, say a word out of place and their boys'll wipe them off. Well, I missed out on that one. She eyed the girl: many a one like that I've seen creeping out of someone else's cabin at three in the morning. An air-hostess, she says she was. You hear all sorts of yarns about them, some say they're good and some say they're goodo. All I know is, I hope she keeps her distance from me.

She lifted the flap and took up place behind the counter, and began to stack the packets of potato chips where they'd be easy to reach. She pretended not to see Sheila strolling in her direction. Wish I'd known she was going to put in an appearance, I'd have put some lipstick on, that's all I need to look my best.

She swung round, braced, as the girl greeted her. "We haven't been favoured with your company for a while. I've forgotten what you look like."

"Oh, didn't Hugh tell you how pooped I've been?" She had one of those silly bleating baby voices copied off Marilyn

Monroe's, she kept her mouth hanging open the same way too. She'd better look out, a bee might fly in, there were half a dozen of them flying round the garbage-tin after the lolly-papers. "By the time I've finished lifting the babies in and out of the water I'm like a wet rag."

Deirdre, her lips tight, kept on stacking the packets.

Sheila hadn't finished cooing. "You're not really cross, are you Deirdre? I've been meaning to ask you both over for dinner."

"We wouldn't have time to come. You're not the only one who's got a job. I start earlier than you most days and finish later. And I work weekends as well."

"Yes, but you aren't dealing with tiddlers."

"Got to psychoanalyze them, have you?" asked Deirdre, serving a double-header cone to one boy and two cans of drink to another, at the same time jamming the beaker up into the mixer.

Sheila laughed, a silly bit of a tinkle, like a cow-bell far off. "No, not really. But—it's just that you can't let up, you've got to get their confidence. They're darlings, though, I've just got to give them a cuddle. Don't you love children?"

Deirdre slammed the money in the register and gave the girl her change before she answered. "I get more than enough of them. If I never set eyes on another kid in my life it'll suit me down to the ground."

Sheila tried another tack. "You haven't been swimming this year, by the look of you Deirdre. Can you swim? If you can't, come over to the pool and I'll teach you."

"We didn't go in for swimming much where I came from. But I can swim enough to save myself if needs be, which is the only reason I see for it. If God meant us to stay in the briny, then he'd have made us all fishes."

Sheila tilted back her head and laughed. Under the counter Deirdre clasped her hands together so she wouldn't give in to the temptation to smack the ninny across the face. She ducked down, away from the sight of her. I've never seen anyone I've taken to less, she thought, and shoved the cartons in place, one on top of the other. Not until she heard Hugh calling did she come up from her hiding-place. Then she stood up, stretching, to hear what he had to say.

He stood there, smiling at her, with one arm thrown casually around Sheila's shoulder. "I'd know that laugh anywhere, Shee. Hi, Deirdre, how's tricks? Come on, Shee, I'll take you up on the Ferris wheel."

"Oo, I hate heights, you know I do. The planes used to terrify me. You'll have to coax me." She let herself be led away, still pouting.

The air was split by a sudden scream. It came from the waxworks. But they were closed—Deirdre looked this way then that, to track down the noise. She pulled up the flap and ran towards the archway. One of the doors stood open: Reg had been in there, tampering with something.

She snapped on the lights. There stood a little boy, a baby almost, about three or four. He was paralysed with fright, holding his breath, the tears pouring down his face. He'd strayed in then—

Deirdre picked him up and put her arms around him, holding him to her. She stood rocking and crooning to him, feeling his heart thump against hers. He went limp, then he struggled against her. His voice came back and he sobbed aloud.

"It's alright. Shh now, don't cry. Where's your mother?" She held him firmly while his little fists beat at her. "Come on, we'll find her for you."

With one hand she turned off the lights and slammed the door. She'd give it to him, that Reggie, poking about where he had no business to be. The child was pulling out of her grasp, pointing to the dodgems.

"Is that where she is? On the dodgems?" His nose was running; she took a handkerchief out of her pocket and wiped it. "Where? Show me."

Still holding him tight she went to the railing. There they were, the two of them, mother and father, ramming each other on the dodgems, laughing like a pair of hyenas; and the kid in her arms trying to escape to get to them.

"Is that your mother?" His yells had died down to hiccups. "She'll only be a minute. Do you want some lollies? No? Alright, we'll just wait."

They waited outside the railing, until the cars shot out their last sparks, then stopped. They all got off, half a dozen scruffy little kids and those two last of all, holding hands and giggling.

"Want another ride?" the fellow asked the girl, as they pushed through the gate.

Deirdre fronted them. "You come here and look after your kid. What d'you think you're doing, the pair of you, letting him roam loose? Ever think there might be perverts around?"

Without knowing she'd raised her voice. Everyone round about turned to stare at her. She put the boy down and he ran to his mother, pushing his head against her jeans while she bent over him.

"What happened, Jase?" Only a kid herself, her skin still pimply, her hair in an untidy pigtail. "It's alright, mummy's got you."

"It's a wonder he didn't fall in the bay. Or run out on the road." Deirdre was hot with anger.

"We were only a minute." The girl picked the little boy up and kissed him. "You're an old silly Jason, getting yourself lost."

"That's the minute that counts. And don't go putting the blame on him, you're the one at fault. I suppose you think there's plenty more where that one came from."

"Oh look here!" The young fellow shaped up to her. "We don't have to listen to that bullshit!"

The girl shushed him. "She's right Paul. We should've had more sense. Thanks, anyway."

"Who'll look after him if his mother won't," said Deirdre, less angry now. "Canoodling's for kids," she threw over her shoulder as she went to the ticket box, where there was a queue waiting, all getting an earful. Reg was behind the counter, taking it all in.

She tore the tickets off roughly, one after another, her face still set. Two teenagers, loitering near, met her eyes. Wagging it from school by the look of them, their raggy grey uniforms covered in grass.

"Wish we hadn't spent our lunch money," one said to the other. "I just feel like a go on the Ferris wheel." Deirdre hesitated, then she began to tear off two tickets.

"Cut that out, Deirdre," called Reg from the kiosk. "We've got to eat too, love."

"A ticket or two won't break us," she retorted, and tore the tickets off. Before he could come back at her she got to him. "What were you doing in the waxworks, Reg? You left the door open."

It was the busiest Friday night they'd had this season: it looked like the beginning of the two or three months when you hardly had time to sit down, you even drank your tea standing up, and fell into bed, asleep before you touched the pillow.

"Looks like we'll be staying open Friday nights from now on, Dee," Reggie called, as he came across the concrete to her. "Got to stay open while they're rolling in. What d'you want for tea? I'll go and get you whatever you fancy. Fish and chips, eh? Or what about a Chiko roll?"

"Oh, I'm not too hungry. Ask if the mangoes are any good. Tell Tony I was the one asking, he'll tell you if they're worth eating yet."

"What about a nice bit of bream? You'll never keep going just on fruit.—Oh, there you are, Tim."

Tim had had a shower and come straight on from work. He was apprenticed to an electrician, that was one of the reasons he was so good with the machines. Nothing bested him. His father was a motor mechanic, they could take any machine apart and put it together again. Reg never let him get out of practice.

"Tim, go and have a look at the lights down at the shooting-gallery, will you? They keep going on and off. Someone'll get their eyes put out if we don't get 'em fixed up."

"You could fix 'em all up with a glass eye, boss," said Tim, cheeky as ever. "Okay, I'm going." He didn't go.

"What's it to be, Dee? Bream? Or a nice bit of flathead?"

"Oh, I got enough of fish when I was working at Harry's."

Reg was sidetracked. "Wonder how he's getting on, old Harry? Never saw a bloke come back so thin from a second honeymoon. Someone told me he's got cancer." His face grew gloomy. "Hope it's not true. Remind me to look him up, will you? Well come on, Deirdre, you still haven't placed your order. You're looking a bit pale these days."

"Oh, get me anything you like, Reg. Just stop making a fuss, that's all. Go on." So he went.

"You must be the most spoiled wife in God's green acre," remarked Tim, whistling while he rolled himself a cigarette. "He loves the ground you tread on, as the saying goes."

"Why wouldn't he? I'm a good workhorse."

"Come off it Deirdre, that's not the reason." He had dirt deep down under the finger-nails of his right hand, but not the left one. He saw her looking, and he held his right hand up for her inspection. "That's the bloke that does all the work, that's why he gets so dirty. The left one's a bludger. I tell you what, Deirdre, if it wasn't for Reg I wouldn't mind having a try for you myself. I've always been partial to Irish girls." His hazel eyes were dancing.

"And Japanese and Greek and—and Portuguese as well," Deirdre shot back. "I've got you summed up, Tim. Where's Nina? I haven't seen her for a while. Not since Hugh's wedding."

"Yeah, it was that wedding started all the strife. She got the idea she was missing out. I had to tell her to get lost in the end. I've got a nice little new chick, wait till you see her. Reg reckons he'll need half a dozen of us on duty weekends from now on.

You wouldn't think a girl'd want to spend her Saturday nights that way, would you? Working round a fun park?"

"Yes I would. Long as you're there."

"Blarney," said Tim, taking a sherbert cone out of a glass jar. "Gosh, I haven't had one of these since I was in napkins. Didn't know you could still get 'em."

Off he went then, a cigarette in one hand and a sherbert cone in the other. He broke off a bit for Rusty, who was busy sniffing out Reggie's trail. Rusty spat it out.

It was nearly dark. She looked out at the night sky, cloudy behind the tall units round the curve of the bay. As she gazed, Tim pulled the master-switch. The sky went out as the lights came on. The southerly blew in, cool on her cheeks, lovely and cool after the heat of the day. The crickets were tuning up, Lord knows where they'd found a place to hide in all that asphalt and concrete. Over in the Norfolk Island pines the little birds were squabbling still, settling down for the night. Deirdre gave a little sigh, for no reason at all she could name. If my feet didn't hurt I might feel more like shaping up to the night in front of me, she thought. Maybe Hugh'll come and take over for a while, and I can put my feet up for half an hour, that'll be enough to pick me up.

Sheila was back, this time by herself. She'd been to the hairdresser's in the interval, and her hair was swirled up as stiff as the mane on a lioness. She had on a different dress, a white one, to show off her tan. Deirdre looked her over. I might try getting a bit of a tan, would it suit me, she wondered. The trouble is I only freckle. But I could try buying myself a few clothes, I've got a better figure than that one, she's beef to the heel like a Hereford steer, for all her waist's so little.

"Hughie's just made me some fairy-floss," said Sheila, sticking her tongue in the pink sugary stuff, licking round her lips. "I'll ruin my figure forever, the calories I've got through tonight."

Reggie was back, with a greasy newspaper full of fish and chips, two mangoes balanced on the top.

Sheila's greedy eyes spotted them. "Oo, mangoes. I didn't know mangoes were in yet."

"Have one," said Reg.

"No." Deirdre leaned over and took them from him. "They're mine."

Sheila's eyes rested on the greasy paper, then flashed up to meet Deirdre's gaze. Then she went back to what she was doing before, flicking her tongue in and out of the paper cone, like a little snake.

"I'll go and see what Hughie's up to," she said, screwing up the paper and leaving it on the counter. "I might get him to win me something from the clowns. They're a scream."

"Take your rubbish with you," Deirdre called after her. She heard, alright, but she kept on going.

Deirdre smouldered. She turned back to the crowd of children waiting. "Who's first?" They all were, or so they said; so she took a guess at it. Funny how they came in spurts: there'd be nobody there, then you turned your back and a dozen lined up. She was flat out serving, too busy to think about eating. The packet of fish and chips got greasier and colder, so she put it on the shelf at the back.

"Who's next?" She said it over and over, hardly even looking into the faces, just the hands shoving money at her. The umpteenth time round it was Sheila who answered, back from the clowns with a fat china pig in her hands. One of these days she'll turn into a china pig herself, fat runs in the family. Deirdre stepped aside to let Hugh bob under the flap, ready to make his usual drink.

"Make me one, darling," purred Sheila.

Deirdre spoke suddenly. "Make me one too. I haven't had any time to eat."

"Oh, didn't you have your fish and chips? I thought you'd be back here tucking into them. And the mangoes."

"I've been too busy."

Sheila gave her tinny little laugh, set the pig down on the

counter, and took the first beaker. Deirdre moved away from her and stood looking out at the bit of bay she could glimpse from a certain spot. She heard the ferry pull in. Backwards and forwards, ten miles over, ten miles back, over and over. Never any difference. We're like a dog on a running-chain, both of us. Or a yo-yo. I never go anywhere but the flat and the park, to and fro.

"The clowns are a scream," Sheila said again. "I love it here, I really do. Do you ever get tired of it, Deirdre?"

Deirdre Kincaid did not bother to answer. It was just put on for Hugh's benefit, all that talk, just an act, everything she said.

"Tell you what you'd like, Shee." Hugh was hollow in the cheeks, thinner than he'd been in October when he'd started work. Deirdre was suddenly concerned; I wonder is she feeding him right? She's so busy looking after her own face, she mightn't have time for anything else.

"What would I like? Tell me," Sheila begged, looking up at him. Everything she did, it was just putting on guiver, there's nothing to her but guiver, thought Deirdre, no wonder I can't stand the sight of her. If I insult her enough, she might stay away. I'll see what I can do. She's nothing to me, why should I put up with her?

"The waxworks!" Hugh exclaimed. "You'll be crazy about them. I'm not saying they're in the same street as the ones up Surfers, still—You haven't opened them much, Deirdre."

"I can't attend to everything. I do the kiosk full time and anything else I'm needed for. I've only got one pair of hands, you know." If her words were rough, her voice came out soft. He meant no harm, Hugh.

"I'll help. I'd like to," said Sheila.

"Tim's new girl's coming in tomorrow."

She wouldn't be silenced. "Can I see the waxworks now? They've got some beauties at Surfers, I couldn't keep away from them."

"I told you I'm too busy. Anyway they're being remodelled,"

Deirdre lied.

"I don't mind." Sheila raised her voice because the merry-go-round had started up again. "I'd love to see them, really."

Deirdre measured her. "I said no. And don't go asking Reggie because I've got the key." All she wants to do is to have her own way, Deirdre was certain of it, then she'll make fun of them. They're my waxworks and I won't have them scorned.

Sheila pouted: it wasn't too often she was crossed. She turned to Hugh for sympathy.

All at once Deirdre couldn't bear any more of it: the noise, the lights, the people pushing around eating and squealing, all of it.

"You take over, Hugh," she said imperiously. She lifted the flap, and stepped out and away. She saw them looking after her and she quickened her steps, in case Reggie came bloodhounding after. Her feet clip-clopped on the concrete as she crossed the strip that led to the wharf. There was the ferry pulled in, the old man hauling the rope from the—what d'you call 'em—bollards—He knew her by sight and he called out to her. She pretended not to hear, if she never heard another human voice in her life, it'd still be too soon. The boat was empty, close on. Down deep near its rusty belly the water came swirling. Bits of rubbish eddied there in the black slime, with dirty bubbles on top. She looked across to the site of the old baths; she remembered them from years back, coming over on the ferry one Christmas, never thinking then she'd be holed up here. Funny what life sends you. Now they were washed away in the big storms. Nothing stays the same.

She set off for somewhere or nowhere, wherever she ended up it didn't matter much, as long as it was a quiet place. The noise of the machines came to her, rising and falling; she hugged the side of the strip away from the fun park. She looked straight ahead in case someone came across to signal to her or detain her. She crossed the road and passed the entrance to the flat, hesitated, then took the street that cut around the back of the township: it was darker and quieter that way. She passed a drunk eating prawns in the gutter, passed two women out walking their dogs on leashes, and another with a Siamese cat. She saw men turning in at their gates, and women looking down from windows. And at last she came out at the far end of the beach, away from the last block of tall units, not short and square like the flats in the back street, but twenty floors, all lit up. She turned her back on them and began to climb the rocks.

There was the sea, before her, below her, the proper sea, not the beach with its dressing-sheds and deck-chairs and rows of garbage-cans. But the black sea stretching wide, rising and falling, joining up with all the waters of the world, those she'd sailed on and those she hadn't. The same sea that ringed the place where she was born. No boat sailed before her eyes as she strained to see, just a hump of sky above and dark sea down under, with the fishes swimming over the wrecks and the bones of the drowned men.

She stood listening to the silence, the waves breaking quietly below her and the calm sky there over her head, with the stars flickering out oehind the bits of blown cloud, and the full moon rising up out of the water on a wash of gold. She waited silent, and the moonlight cut a path across the sea and lit up the deep water, breaking below the rocks where she stood, not so far down as she'd thought. It sounded as if it was chuckling, laughing at her, calming her down: sh-oosh—and it chuckled again—sh-oosh. The sea-wind was strong and salty, blowing in from the north-east, cleaner and clearer than the one that blew across the bay. She felt herself calm, as if she'd been washed clean of what ailed her. What did ail me, then?—Nothing. I ought to get away from the place more, I let it get on my nerves, that's all. When the season's over I'll go somewhere, not with Reg, somewhere by myself near the sea, and I'll lay down quiet in the sun till it soaks through me. And I'll know by the end of the summer what's likely to happen next. I'll be given a sign, go or stay. Maybe I'm healed now, without even knowing it. Maybe I've served my time in limbo. I'll see.

6

Deirdre was sleeping when Reggie tapped at the door. The knock made its way into her sleep; she moved and ground her teeth and burrowed into her pillow.

"Deirdre, wake up. Wake up, love." The voice kept it up till she had no choice but to open her eyes and come back to the world she'd closed them on.

Reggie was standing by the bed, in the moth-eaten old dressing-gown he'd pulled out of the pensioners' rag-bag, again. He was holding a tray in his hands, squaring off, not that he needed to, he'd done nothing wrong last night, or ever, for that matter. She'd heard him open the door and peer in at her; then close it quietly so he wouldn't disturb her.

"Your headache better? Tell you what, the place didn't seem the same without you. Hugh and Sheila weighed in, but the two of them together didn't make up." He put the tray down on the frayed cane table, and pulled the Chinese screen round to where he could look at it. "You're a sight for sore eyes, the pair of you. You curled up in bed there and the screen next to you. Wish I could paint."

Deirdre pulled her naked arms down under the sheet, stretching her legs luxuriously out in the big bed, curling and uncurling her toes. Sleeping all by yourself in a double bed, it gives you plenty of room. She yawned. "What's the time, Reg?"

"Where'd you get to last night?" he quizzed her. "I came over here half a dozen times looking for you."

"Nowhere. I just went for a walk. I got fed up with the noise."

"Dee." He sat down, catching hold of her foot that she'd poked out by mistake. "Can I move in here? I hate sleeping by myself. I wake up at night and think of all my mates dropping off one by one. I reckon if I could put out my hand and find you there I'd get off to sleep again."

"Try Rusty," she answered, after a moment.

"No, I'm not kidding. I wouldn't try any funny stuff, love."

She wouldn't look at his face. "You couldn't. Even if you wanted."

"I like company. I never get enough of your company, I've told you that before."

"We get enough of one another all day long." She hardened herself against the grieving note in his voice.

"You speak for yourself. I was good for nothing last night till I looked in and saw you curled up."

"Reg I told you I've got to get my sleep. I can't stand being grabbed." She was tense, but she tried to turn it into a joke. "I don't want any gorilla-holds in the night, that's all there is to it."

"I won't even get a little monkey-grip on you, I swear on the Bible. I'd just like to put out my hand once in a while—"

"That's just what I meant. I need my sleep. You get about four hours, then you start revving up for the day. I'd be like a rag after one night of it." She was suddenly angry: he had no right to make her feel a heel. "Come on Reg, we know where we stand. Let's leave it at that. You're dead in the crotch, and I'm dead in the—" She looked at his face, all woe-begone, and she sighed. She hated hurting him.—"heart," she finished.

He was silent. Then he got off the ropes, the way he always did. "You dead," he scoffed. "You've got more fire in you than any woman born." He got up and shifted the screen forward a bit, then back. He blinked a couple of times and gave a sniff, pretending to examine the lacquer. "The lacquer's cracking in the corner, that's why I got it for a song—" He swung round, all at once fierce. "When I think what I got cheated out of—Wish I could get hold of those bastards that put the boot in. I'd have their livers, one by one."

Deirdre sat up, pulling the sheet round her shoulders, drawing up her knees, propping her elbow on them. She'd always been curious, it was one of the few things Reggie had kept to himself. But this morning he'd tell her anything she wanted to know, and suddenly she was resolved to find out.

"How did it happen, Reg?" she whispered, soft as that sly-boots, Sheila.

"Well, Dee, I don't think it makes me look too good, not that I'm ashamed of anything I did, the little monkey asked for it. She was at the bottom of everything."

"A girl monkey?" Deirdre wanted to laugh at his face, so comical and full of woe. That Reg, he'd never be the hero in a tragedy, he'd got the wrong kind of looks for it.

"Yeah, you can put it like that. A cute little thing she was, full of tricks. Sixteen or so—well, maybe not quite. She was a swimmer."

"Swimmer?" All the stories about the Kincaids, they ended up watery, or round the water's edge. "I can guess the rest," she told him. "Who did you over, the brother or the father?"

"The whole bloody lot of them. It was murder." His eyes were hard, his mouth twisted in a snarl. "They waited for me out the back of the R.S.L. in the dark under the trees. They left me a bloody pulp."

Her heart was hot with pity. Poor old guy.

"She made a dead set at me, Dee, that's the truth, I swear to God. Always asking me to rub her shoulders, well a man's only flesh and blood." He paused, then went on. "Things weren't too good at home, the wife had taken the little girl off to stay with her mother, she said I was never home, she might as well be in England—"

"Were you? Hardly ever home?"

"What? No."

Deirdre leaned forward. "Did she look like Sheila, that girl that chased you? I bet she did."

Reg stared at her. His face lost its terrible bitter lines. "Yeah, funny you saying that, she did a bit. Well they beat hell out of me, the bunch of 'em, and they left me there. Next thing the sawbones took over. They put a steel plate here and a wire doover there, and they patched me up after they finished chopping me about. Trouble was, one of the bits they chopped out I couldn't really spare." He put his hand on the counterpane over her knee. "When I think what they done me out of I could howl like a mangy dog."

Deirdre was silent, trying to think of something to say, anything to end the silence. "I wouldn't have married you then," she said. Then she was sorry, thinking it might make him feel worse.

He jumped up, rocking the screen. With one of his big scratched paws he righted it. "Yes you would. I'd have chased you round the world and back again. Like the sheik of Araby your love belongs to me."

All at once he'd had enough of sadness, and he turned back into a clown. He began to sing, "At night when you're asleep into your tent I'll creep—"

She began to laugh. He could always set her laughing. "You just try." Under the bedclothes she pulled up her shoulder-straps that she'd pulled off her shoulders in the night. "You sleep in your own tent, Ali. Hand over the tray, will you?"

He felt the teapot. "It's cold. I'll make you some more."

"Don't bother," said Deirdre. "I'm not too fussy, as long as it's wet it'll do. Did you drink your orange juice? Don't make a fuss, Reg, I'll take the will for the deed. Go and shave. We've got a long day ahead of us."

He put the tray on her knees, kissed the top of her head and went shambling off, looking every hour of his age, fifty two, was he?

"Reg," she called after him, suddenly ashamed of herself, always on the taking end of the arrangement. He'd been better to her than anyone else in the world. She'd have to talk softer to him, it was the least she could do. "You're a good man Reg, don't think I don't know what you're worth. I was lucky you chose me."

7

If November was busy, then what did you call December? All the boats that pulled in were chock-a-block with trippers, mostly children with parents, now that the school holidays had come. More children were emptied out of the tall units where their grandparents lived.

"We're coining money hand over fist." Reg was gloating more each day as the takings kept rising. "If it keeps on like this we'll have to put someone else on. Trouble is, where d'you get an honest kid? There's so much free money floating round the booths, kids, they're not saints. Tim and Bob, they were finds. Get hold of one of those light-fingered young blokes, he'd be into the cash like a chicken into—" He stopped. "Best we do it ourselves, Dee, long as we can manage it. I'll get hold of Hugh, if I pay him I might get a bit of work out of him."

"Just as long as you don't ask that Sheila. I can't stand a bar of her."

"Oh, she's a nice little thing. But I won't if you don't want her," he added hastily. "We'll manage, I s'pose. Hugh can do with a bit of extra money."

The whole week now was a string of Saturday arvos: so much to do that half the time she felt like a merry-go-round herself, always on the go, giddy with chasing her own tail.

All the kids wanted to see the waxworks. Every now and then she put Jenny, Bob's girl friend, in the kiosk in her place, and went to open up. She wasn't much to look at, Jenny, but she was a good worker. Deirdre didn't do it often, just once in a while. She liked to see that they were all in there, waiting for her, all those wax dummies. Call it queer if you like, but that was the way she felt.

This time it was half a dozen little boys she had in tow. They all trooped after her and waited under the archway. A pack of young hooligans they were, all ages from five or six to twelve, all dressed in grubby jeans and worn-down sneakers, their cheeks bulged out with lollies or chewing gum.

"Come on then," she said.

They were all impressed by the first one.

"That's the one I like best," said Deirdre. "It makes me feel sad, though." She gazed at their small faces, drained of colour in the artificial light, their wide-open eyes. Little boys, they get you in. She stole a glance at the wax boy. Yes, he was still there, still pleading.

She wheeled round and they followed her, chattering and eating, lagging behind to goggle when they felt inclined. A red-head, a toughie of about twelve or so, was a bit more of a wake-up than the rest of them. He started to sling off about the broken guillotine.

"They're not near as good as the ones at King s Cross," he was bragging, as if the whole of King s Cross belonged to him. "The ones there give you the creeps. I reckon they're robbers here to make you pay at all."

Deirdre was charmed by his cheeky grin, his red hair standing on end, the peeling nose plastered with zinc cream, most of all the cocky tilt of his head.

"Look out you don't turn out a robber yourself. You've got a face like Ned Kelly, and you know what happened to him. I bet you're as game as Ned Kelly too."

"Come off it, missus," he muttered, looking down at his dirty sneakers with the laces dangling.

She was sorry when they came to the last one and she had to surrender them. I wish I owned them all, she thought, and that's the truth. They stood in front of the headless woman, snuffling and chewing.

"She might have been born like that," someone suggested.

"Oh I don't think so," said Deirdre, going across to the switch. "Come on now, all you bruisers and I'll give you an ice-cream on the house."

"On the house?" they asked.

"She means free," said the red-head. She felt him bump against her. "Sorry I give you cheek, missus," he said under his breath, to her alone.

Deirdre bent down and whispered to him. He smelled of young skin and peppermint. "You were right, they are crummy. But keep it dark, will you?"

She closed the door and they flocked after her to the kiosk, reaching out sticky fingers to grab their ice-creams, but not forgetting to say thank you. She smiled after them. Either you liked little boys or they'd—what was the word—petrify you. The boy with red hair turned to wave to her and she waved back.

Hugh was standing a little way off with Benny, the one he used to train with, the one that nearly made it to the Games, but just missed out at the end. Hugh was sounding off about using the media. Benny was sounding off about the need for educating the illiterate masses. If I didn't know them, thought Deirdre in amusement, I'd say what a pair of pain in the necks. Benny was trying, a bit late in the day, to get into P.E. teaching.

"Twenty two, that's not too late. Wouldn't mind doing it myself for a crust." That was Hugh.

"Why don't you?" That was Ben.

"Oh." Hugh had to think. "Well I've got a job. And there's Sheila."

They walked away, still talking, moving with the same easy stride. They were off to have a go at the rifles.

Reg and Tim were sweating over the motor that always chose the busiest time to play up. Jacky Mobbs, full of free whisky, came up from the office to offer some free advice. He turned up whenever it suited him, to listen to the races and get through half a bottle of whisky and to touch Reg for whatever he could get out of him. Nobody knew where he lived, round Kensington somewhere, Reg thought. He was always hanging round the race-tracks, picking up tips and handing them on.

He still had time to put in today, so it looked as if he hadn't put the fangs in yet. He jerked his thumb after Hugh and his mate, the two of them just disappearing down the alleyway.

"Hugh's been fixing milk shakes for himself and his cobber, I see." He had eyes in the back of his head.

"Why not?" Deirdre flashed at him. "He's entitled to it if he wants to. He's a big help to Reg."

Jacky Mobbs rubbed his chin. He was forever scratching at himself; he had a ton of filthy habits, picking his nose, that was another one, scratching his behind, spitting—He was getting ready to spit now, but he stopped himself in time.

"I might get you a spittoon for Christmas, Jacky. It'd keep your room clean."

"Yeah, you do that, Deirdre. What's he do to help, young Hughie?"

"Oh, a million things. He hoses the place down and repairs the dodgems. He works in the kiosk to give me a break. He takes the money for the clowns—That enough for you?"

"Yeah, he's not a bad kid. He's tight though, he always was. Even when he was a nipper he had a scorpion in his pocket. I reckon he's still got his playlunch money."

Deirdre fired up. She looked the old sponger up and down, he'd never done an honest day's work in his life, his face red from the whisky he'd never paid for, his strands of grey hair spread out over his pink skull to make them go farther.

"What would you have him do, empty his pockets out all over Australia like his father, so's he could get to fifty without a rahzoo to his name. If it hadn't been for a lucky horse—"

"I gave him that horse," snarled Jacky.

"Maybe you did and maybe you didn't. All the spongers run from their holes when they see him coming."

"Are you referring to me, Deirdre, by any chance?"

"If the cap fits you wear it, Jacky Mobbs!"

"Seven pineapple splices," somebody called, and Deirdre plunged her hand in and dragged them out, five six seven. "Eighty four cents," she said.

Reggie hopped down from the platform, holding the biggest

spanner she'd ever seen in her life. He'd come to smooth things down.

"Don't pick a fight with her, Jacky. She's got a wild Irish temper hid under those black curls."

Deirdre rounded on him. "I've got no temper left, Reg. I killed it years ago and shovelled it under."

Jacky Mobbs was pretending to laugh, but his eyes, as he raked her over, were hard as stones. "Get the hurdy-gurdy going, Reg?"

"Just about. Till the next time. It needs breaking up for scrap, that's all it's good for. You wait and see, one of these days I'll come home with one that'll knock your eyes out."

She turned her back on them. Reggie and merry-go-rounds, they made a combination she didn't feel up to today. She heard Reggie talking to Jacky in a whisper nearly as loud as anyone else's shout.

"You think twice before you take a young wife, Jacky," he was saying. "They're like a ball of fire, they'll scorch the soul-case out of you."

She couldn't be bothered taking him up on it, he'd only talk his way out of it anyway.

"Deirdre. Dee." He wouldn't stop till she turned to him. "Why don't you get yourself a new dress? If we're going to have a Christmas party you might as well be belle of the ball. Not that you need it to put everyone else in the shade."

"I might do that, Reg," she answered him. It might be nice to get herself dolled up for once, see if her looks had forsaken her. Overalls, they didn't do much for your beauty.

8

She knew the dress shop to go to, the one two streets up. She'd heard Sheila say it was the best shop in Brightsea, but the prices were red-hot, too high for poor little me, as she put it.

It's two years since I bought anything new, so I don't care what it costs me, she decided, and stepped firmly over the threshold. There wasn't much to see, just grey velvet curtains and two spindly grey chairs, and a grey-haired woman who shimmied out, too proud to do more than half smile. Deirdre saw the snooty glance at her overall, but it didn't get her down: in the pocket she had two hundred dollars, you could get a lot of dress for that much, even these days. She looked the woman straight in the eye.

"Pick me a winner, will you?" She watched while the woman in black pulled back the curtains. "Oo," she said, catching her breath at the array of silks and beautiful embroidered cottons. One of them was dark brown with pink roses and green velvet ribbons. "I guess this one's too young for me," she said, fingering it. "I've got two hundred dollars to spend."

The woman smiled at her then, nice blue eyes she had, yellow in the teeth though.

"No. But it wouldn't catch your particular look. It's anybody's dress. Any pretty woman's. You've got a beautiful carriage. What are you, ten or twelve? Are you thin across the chest? Slip off that overall and let me see whether you need to be covered up." So Deirdre did as she was told, feeling like a school kid. "No, you're just right. Lovely milky skin. Are you Irish?" She rifled through the row on the rack and brought out a long gold dress. "Did you say it was for evening?"

Deirdre nodded. "A party. I might only wear it the once, but I'd like to look—I'd like to make an impression. Yes, I'm Irish, can you tell? My voice, is it? I thought I'd lost the brogue."

"No, it's still there. There's something in the planes of the face, too. Slip it on. Are you wearing rouge?"

"No, that's the colour I am."

She slipped into the dress and the woman zipped it up. They turned together and looked at the woman in the long glass, with gold straps over her milky shoulders and the neck of a queen.

"I knew it was right." The woman was pleased, almost skiting you could say. "It brings out the gold lights in your eyes. Wear gold sandals, will you? Coil your hair up off your neck. It's a shame not to show it."

"I do. But when I'm working it keeps coming down." She was dawdling, looking at herself in the glass, amazed to see that she could look like that. "I don't want to take it off," she murmured, sliding her hands down over her hipbones, feeling the slippery silk. She had to force herself to unzip it. "I haven't bothered much about my appearance."

"I can see that," the shop woman said with a little smile. "Then of course you don't need to. I wish I had the job of dressing you." She was folding the dress in masses of white tissue paper, for two hundred dollars they threw that in. "I'd burn that pink overall."

Deirdre laughed, still excited by what she'd seen in the glass. "That's my tools of trade, as you might put it. I couldn't make fairy-floss in gold silk. I'll just have to be like Cinderella. Do a lightning change act, I mean, just for the night." She did up the buttons on her overall.

"I hope it brings you good luck," said the woman, taking the money, handing over the box. "Oh, you're twenty dollars short." Her voice was sharp. "No, it's all here. Good luck."

9

Some party it was going to be. Lobsters and cold chicken and half a dozen different kinds of salad. A trifle so tall and wide you could hardly jump over it. A fruit punch, so much rum in it that one whiff nearly knocked you out.

In other words, Reg was at it again. When she protested that they'd just finished with one party he stood his ground. He'd do the cooking—didn't he run a catering business up there at Broken Hill. Alright, it was years back, but you never lost the knack of it—

"You never told me, Reg."

"No, I got lots of secrets still locked up inside me. I'm like that crafty old bugger in the Arabian Nights, I just let 'em out one at a time."

"She was a girl that told the stories, I think."

"Doesn't matter. Now come on Dee, if I do the cooking and pay the bill, where's your gripe? All you got to do is sit up there like the queen of the whole shebang."

She gave in. "Just one thing, Reg. Don't have as many as last time. We were nearly squashed to death. Specially if you're not going to open the park up."

"No bloody way. The dodgems haven't been the same since. You can blow tripe out of the kids, but you can't say boo to your son's pals. It's alright, Dee, we'll only have a dozen or so."

That was how it was all decided. And he'd done what he promised, teed it all up, even to the music.

The day before the party, a covered van pulled up at the pier, and two old fellows climbed out and fell on Reggie's neck. It was always like that, he had people turning up from Darwin or Alice or God knows where. These two were furniture removers. Reg left with them to help them up the stairs with the present he'd got her for Christmas, or so he said. He came back two hours later, the worse for wear. Nothing would do but that she'd go with him to look them over, those presents.

He opened the door of the flat with a flourish, then barred the way. "Open your mouth and close your eyes and see what God'll send you.—That's what my mother used to say when I was a little bloke. Ready?"

Deirdre closed her eyes. She put out her hands and felt wood with one hand, and something cold, steel, with the other. She opened her eyes and looked with horror at the gun. A gun? For a Christmas present?

"I ought to shoot you with it," she said, furiously. "What sort of present's that? That your idea of a joke, Reg?"

He took the gun from her limp hands. "Well, that's not your real present. But you might be glad of it, you never know with all these prowlers around. I picked it up cheap, it's a beautiful job. I'll teach you how to use it, you can keep it loaded for an emergency. If you won't come with me on my trips I'll have to teach you to protect yourself. Close your eyes again."

"I've had enough of jokes. What is it this time?"

He pointed to the corner of the room, how she'd missed seeing it she couldn't imagine. With the help of his two old cobbers and a skinful of beer he'd managed to squeeze a pianola in there.

"There you are. Music on tap. All you've got to do is pedal away. Like it?"

It was lovely, old Italian walnut and two gold candle-holders. She ran her hands over the smooth wood.

"Complete with rolls," said Reggie with great pride. "Thought you'd like it. It's got a history, that pianola. Belonged to a Q.C.—K.C. as they used to be called—fifty years back. His daughter wouldn't part with it. But she died last week and old Stan, he rang me up and asked did I want it."

"Who's old Stan? No, don't tell me," she added hastily. "Does it go?"

"Does it go?" He pulled over the stool, gave it a twirl, sat down, rubbed his hands together and began to pedal. "I know this one," he hollered over the noise, plink-plonk. "My canary's got circles under his eyes, it's called." He didn't know it too well, only a word here and there, but at least he could sing in tune, that was one blessing, considering that he'd be doing the canary act non-stop from now on. "Like your present, love?"

"Oh Reg!" She gave him a quick hug and moved quickly away. "You bought it for yourself, tell the truth."

"Yes, I know. But there's a couple of fancy candles wedged down inside the holders there."

Slowly she unwrapped the bills he'd poked down inside the holders. It was a lot of money, a thousand dollars or more. She didn't bother to count it: money, that was one thing that didn't bother her.

"I got myself a new dress. I don't need this, Reg," she told him. "Put it away for yourself."

"You've earned every cent of it and more, Dee. Now you won't grudge me a bit of a rort, will you?"

"No," she answered, looking down at the money, folding and unfolding it. She didn't need it and she didn't want it. "I'll put it away in case we go broke."

He was pedalling away, singing Am I Blue, whistling it when he forgot the words. She looked at him, his hair turning grey, coarse hair growing out of his battered ears, his blunt fingers pretending to play the notes that were playing by themselves. He was worth more than any fellow she'd ever known; pity you couldn't give love like a present to the one that needed it most. Doesn't go like that, though, just the opposite.

10

Christmas night they turned it on. Deirdre hurried through her shower, pulling on an old white towelling robe over her underclothes. She sat in front of the spotted mirror of the dressing-table, while Reg fussed about with the nuts and the olives. He had himself laired up in a sort of safari suit. It might last out the night before he put his brand on it.

She coiled up her hair and she reddened her lips. Too bright, maybe? She'd see when she put the dress on. She slipped it over her head, tilting the glass, standing back to see what it told her. She drew in a sharp breath of pleasure. If I'm not a beauty then I'm the next thing to it. Fancy that. She sat down, quite winded by the discovery.

Behind her, Reggie loomed up in the glass. "Gawd Almighty! It's the Queen of Sheba in all her regalia. Well Dee—" He put his hands on her shoulders, warm on top of the gold straps. "All I can say is—you scrub up well. Skin like silk you've got, love." He took his hands away, but stayed there, looking at her.

"Oh bugger it," he growled, after a moment. "That's the story of my life. Too much too late or too little too soon or however they put it. Tell you what, you need a full-length mirror. I've got one in the office, I'll lug it over for you."

"The trick one? It'll chop me up then mirror me twenty times over." She laughed aloud, exhilarated.

"All the better." He came and kissed her on the cheek, a quick kiss, but sloppy. "I better go and see to the keg."

Just in time. The first-comers were toiling up the stairs, Jacky Mobbs—who else?—with the bloke who'd put Reggie on to the pianola. Deirdre stood up, smoothing the dress over her hips and belly. She came to greet them. As Stan pumped her hand up and down she heard the next lot clattering up. Someone was laughing, Tim by the sound of it, yes Tim, with a tall skinny blonde she'd never set eyes on before. When he spotted Deirdre he came leaping over. He took her hands and swung her this way then that, like the first steps of a dance.

"Gee, Deirdre," he said. "You take my breath away." He wasn't joking either. Suddenly shy, she found no words to answer him. Clothes, you wouldn't think they'd make that much difference; but they did. "I'm lovesick," he whispered in her ear, before he went back to that lamp-post nearly six foot high that Reggie was chatting up.

He came back again to her. "I'll come and play my guitar outside your balcony window tonight," he promised, maybe meaning it, maybe not. You couldn't tell with Tim.

Reggie was scooping out the punch, wetting his own whistle along the way. "Reggie's own brand. Reggie's calypso cocktail. Guaranteed to set you swinging from the ceiling. Come on Jenny, try a sample, you'll never be the same girl after." He was making a big fuss of Jenny, done up in turquoise frills and plainer than ever, but so nice it didn't matter.

And here was Ben, filling up the door, pushing a girl in front of him like a hostage in a Western. No sooner had he left the doorway vacant than Sheila came to fill it, you couldn't miss her in her long flounced pyjamas all the colours of the rainbow, waves of scent coming out from her, every inch of her arms jangling with bracelets.

"You splurged!" She narrowed her eyes at Deirdre, before she turned her back.

Where was Hugh, then? He was always on time. Maybe he wasn't coming at all. Then she saw him stepping out of the dining-room with a stack of pianola rolls; somehow she'd missed him while she was doing the rounds.

He stopped dead when he saw her. "Hello Deirdre." He stood still, looking at her. "I hardly knew you."

"What d'you think of your stepmother, Hughie?" called the loudmouth she was tied up to. "Beautiful—or not?"

"Beautiful!" Hugh exclaimed. Then away he went.

Two more of his friends, or Sheila's maybe, were busting in

through the door, calling out to Sheila as if it was her place and her party. They've got hide, those young ones, thought Deirdre, letting her glance drift over them and away.

Voices rose and fell. The punch bowl was emptied. Reg poured more in from a plastic bucket.

"Hope that's not the one we keep the sheep-dip in," bawled Bob, not drunk, but not too sober, either.

"I bought it fresh from Woolworths, so help me God," Reg swore.

Stan and Jacky Mobbs were sitting side by side on the sofa, eating their way through a plate of asparagus rolls. Trust Jacky Mobbs.

Two more of Reggie's mates, both of them strangers to her, came stumbling over the threshold, bottles of oysters sticking out of their pockets. One was holding a carton of beer and the other a box of chocolates.

"This where Reg Kincaid hangs out?"

"It certainly is." Reg came charging over to hug them. "You found your way alright after all, eh? Still on your legs," he added, no doubt to encourage them, as they stood there, weaving. "Come and meet my wife. Well, here they are, Deirdre, two of the best blokes I ever worked with. Don and Nugget, meet Deirdre."

Deirdre let them pump her hands and smiled into their faces. "I'm glad you could come."

"Pleased to meet you," said Don, handing over the chocolates.

Nugget was drunker, not too sure of what he was saying. "Thought your wife was called Dulcie, Reg."

Reg didn't even blink. "She went back to England donkeys' years ago. This one's the new model."

"She's a Rolls-Royce," said Don.

"Another Irishman," Deirdre sighed.

Reg clapped him over the shoulder, and righted him just in time. "We're both Scotch. We're both dinkum two generations back, then we're Scotch. Talking of Scotch, what'll it be?"

"We brought our own," bragged Nugget, holding up a dozen beer cans in a carton.

Someone was playing the pianola hell for leather. Benny was singing Bye Bye Blackbird. Everyone had a go at the chorus.

Deirdre Kincaid had the strangest feeling of having been there before, years back. She shook her head to clear it.

"What's wrong, Dee? Got a headache?" Reg, on his way to the keg, stopped at her side.

"No. I just had the funniest feeling that I'd been here before. As if it all happened before."

"That's called deejar voo," said Reg. "Well it's only three months or so since the last one."

"Where's the asparagus rolls?" Hugh had come up behind them. "I told you to make a stack of them, dad." Tall and lanky in his cream slacks, his shoulders broad under his cream shirt, he waited beside her, clapping his arm round Reggie's shoulders, but smiling down at her.

Deirdre moved three paces over to Jacky Mobbs, and picked up the plate that had been piled high a few minutes before. "Six left," she said. She replaced it with a tray of sausage-rolls. "Swap."

Jacky wasn't too happy about the changeover. "Where's your mob tonight, Deirdre?" he asked her, very innocent, like fun. "Can't see any of them round. Left 'em in Ireland to get on with the fighting, did you?"

Reggie bristled. A glass of beer in his hand, he came over to Jacky. For a moment it looked as if Jacky'd get it in the face; then he chuckled. "She's got no need of friends. I'm her husband and her boss and her best-loved friend, eh, Deirdre? The best day of my life was the one she said yes, that's the gospel truth."

"Half your luck," Stan sang out, downing his beer.

In his basket Rusty was growling to himself. No doubt the poor thing can hardly breathe, thought Deirdre, all at once finding herself short of air. So many people. She went out to the balcony and tugged at the window until it creaked and at last opened. Tim came out to stand next to her. She knew what he was going to say before he spoke. She'd seen his stewed eyes earlier in the evening, six beers back.

"You look beautiful, Deirdre. If you weren't the boss's wife you'd never get away from me."

There in the half-dark, Deirdre met his gaze levelly. "But I am." Funny that, she thought, I've never had any time for sandy men. Black ones and golden, they're the ones that caught my eye.

She turned abruptly back to the window. "Go and play, Tim," she said, over her shoulder. "There's your girl friend in there pining for you."

She was too, Tim peered in and gave a groan. "One day I'll get myself a bird who doesn't keep tabs on me."

Grumbling and belching, Tim went back to pick up his guitar and soon there was one more noise added to the talking and laughing and tinny thumping of the pianola. It turned into a contest. Half of them chimed in with Tim and the other half stayed with the pianola.

Deirdre leaned out, sniffing up the cool air, full of seaweed and petrol and frangipani. Out there in the dark was the long stretch of bay, all lights on one side, black hills on the other, with just a sprinkle of houses, the dark bulk of the jetty buildings making a frame as she looked out over them. The moon made a track across the water, close on full. Funny how it came up orange, then got paler as it rose higher. There'd be a reason for that, if you only knew it. Honeymoon, maybe that meant pale as honey, then again it could be sweet as honey.

The step at her side, that step, it was Hugh. Her heart gave a leap. She swivelled and smiled full into his serious face.

"You gave me a start," she said, at last. "I was miles away."

"Great party." He leaned against the window in the half-light, smiling. "But I've had too much to drink. I'm not used to it. That's a pretty dress. You look lovely."

She glowed. "Do I? I hoped you'd like it. It makes me feel—"

"What?" He leaned towards her. She did not answer, but breathed in, waiting.

The pianola snatched him away from her. He was listening while the whole room bawled out a song she'd always hated, I'll take you home again Kathleen. Tears sprang to her eyes. She tried to stop, but they spilled down her cheeks.

"Are you crying, Deirdre?" he asked uncertainly, coming closer. "What's wrong? Are you homesick?"

"No, I never think of home. Else I'd die." She was at a loss, why was she crying? She couldn't stop trembling. She brushed the tears away with the back of her hand. "It's all the smoke," she whispered, still holding herself in waiting.

"All in the dark, you two." Reg stood between them, holding out a plate of Christmas cake. "Hear that song love. I swear I will, one of these days."

"Everyone keeps talking about Ireland. All those songs they sing, they're just malarky as far as I'm concerned." She was still trembling, but with anger. "I hate it. I hate everything that happened to me there. I never want to go back as long as I live."

They were quiet now, and so was she, her outburst done. Tim began a fresh blast, "You couldna hear the music for the swishing—", dahdumming the words not fit to be heard in mixed company: that didn't leave him much to go on with. Deirdre could see him where he sat, so hot and drunk, strumming away like crazy. She felt it would take nothing to make her start screaming or sobbing or worse.

"That no-hoper!" Reg frowned, while he gave a snort of laughter. "I told him to keep it clean."

Hugh's face, as the light caught it, was dark with anger. So he'd heard the song somewhere before, though you'd hardly believe he'd sit still to hear it to the end.

He thrust his way back into the room and yanked the guitar out of Tim's hands. "What sort of song's that to sing in front of ladies!"

Sheila was stretched out at Tim's feet, leaning on her elbows, sucking on a cherry from her drink, wearing the upturned glass on her head like a cap, egging Tim on.

"Come on Sheila. We're going home. Get your top."

"Oh no," she groaned.

"Come on, before the party gets any rougher." He stood in front of her scowling, not budging an inch.

"Good on you, son," called Jacky Mobbs. "You stand up for what you believe in."

Deirdre left the balcony. She stood at Hugh's side, touched his elbow lightly. "Don't go Hugh," she begged, speaking low, so that no one else would hear her. "It wouldn't be the same without you."

He ignored her. He'd had more to drink than she'd realized. His speech was thick and slurred. "Hurry up Sheila, before I pick you up and carry you."

"Real Valentino stuff," called one of the old fellows, swallowing the last of his oysters.

With an angry shrug Sheila got up and flounced off into the bedroom to get her jacket.

"There's a gun in there next to the wardrobe," called Reg. "Go on, shoot him, Hugh, he doesn't deserve to live."

Hugh started after Sheila. He took the gun from the corner of the bedroom, where it was leaning against the wall. He picked it up, running his hands over the barrel, then aiming it at Timmy. Then he put it down again and came back to the party.

"Does it work?" asked Benny.

"You bet it does. I got it for Deirdre for when I'm away. So if any of you young blokes get any ideas about climbing up on to her balcony, you better have another think. I'll be teaching her how to handle it."

All the drunks hooted with laughter. The pianola got going again. Sheila was ready to go, still sulky, and Hugh had her by the arm, steering her towards the door, while she grumbled and pulled back. He really meant it then: there was no keeping him. Deirdre waited for him to speak to her.

"Bye dad. Bye Deirdre. Merry Christmas." And that was all.

It was about three in the morning when the last of them said goodbye. Stan decided he was too crook to drive, so he'd doss down on the sofa, if they'd have him.

Deirdre took it all in: the upside-down room, the food and drink mashed-up and spilled wherever you looked. Let the cockroaches have a feast tonight, if they came searching. As far as she was concerned it could wait till morning, all of it. She poured herself half a glass of milk, hesitated, then filled it up with whisky. I don't want to be awake tonight, she thought, it might put me to sleep. She felt wretched, like something the cat had found in the gutter and dragged in. Am I blue, as the song said—what did it say?—if your plan with your man done fell through.—

She was—she didn't know what she was—She felt herself—splintered—yes, that was the way she felt, all in splinters.

When she sank back into her bed, her head seemed to follow a long time after, as if it didn't belong on her body at all. Maybe I'm drunk, she thought, what did I have? A cup of that punch and a couple of beers. And then that whisky. I'm not much of a one for booze, maybe it went to my head. Yes, and there was that gin and ginger Reggie brought me over. Did I have anything to eat, no I didn't.

Her eyelids grew thick and her body light, that meant she'd drift off, thank God, not tossing the way she did, night after night, that terrible time. I won't think of it, no I won't, let sleep take me, carry me—

She slept. In her sleep she moved and turned her head and muttered. Beneath her feet sprang grass, soft as feathers, and it seemed she was lying in feathers, then it changed, she was lying in grass, green grass. No longer alone, she lay back; and she held out her arms to the boy running towards her, faster, till with one last leap he threw himself down at her side. He clasped her to him, then he let her go. He took her hand and gently straightened her cupped fingers. On her finger he put a ring, he'd come from the fair, he'd won it there, and come speeding to put it on her finger. It was green and gold, with two snakes entwined. His hand closed over hers, and the face with the eyes so blue and the rough black hair was close to hers, and full of tenderness. She turned on her side, pulling him to her, straining him close.

"Dermond," she cried, the name coming out of her like a gasp for life. She put her hands behind his head, drawing his face to hers, kissing his lips, closing her eyes. And when he pulled away she opened her eyes to look at him. But the face she saw was a stranger's, no, not a stranger's—it was Hugh's face that looked into hers, his eyes smiling back at her, his lips that she'd kissed.

11

So hot. So hot that you felt yourself dried-out and puckered-up by the end of the day. The water steamed up when Reg hosed the concrete; by the time he turned the hose off it was close on dry. They never stopped pouring off the ferry or running back from the ocean. They never stopped eating and drinking and shouting and squabbling and tearing from one ride to another. The merry-go-round never stopped going round and round, and the Ferris wheel never stopped going up and round and down and round, over and over and over. The dodgems never stopped crashing and the rifles never stopped cracking. The new machines, the peepshows, nothing much to peep at but girls getting undressed, they had queues lining up for a look. The cash-register jingled, and the lavatory-paper got torn off. The rubbish got thrown down and swept up again. Every day. Every night.

And the sun never stopped beating down. Even in the shade it was stifling. Rusty lay wherever he could find a pool of shade, getting up to groan and flop down in another place just as hot. Reggie had given him a bit of a shearing, not too expert, one half of his rump hadn't got finished. One thing Reg hadn't been was a barber, by the look of the job. Fairy-floss and chips were spilled and trodden flat. There was always someone dropping ice-cream and someone else skidding on it. Every day some stupid kid went on the merry-go-round too soon after a milk shake. Sometimes they got off in time. Sometimes they didn't make it, and the horse copped it. The smell of disinfectant was mixed with the smell of sweat and scent. The waters of the bay slapped against the scrap of sand, dark and oily, with bits of charred wood floating about, and chocolate wrappers, and sometimes a bit of plank or a dead mutton-bird.

Once a little girl, scrambling down to the sand to rescue her sun hat, found a bit of rubber floating.

"Look, mummy, I've found a funny little balloon."

"Give me the nasty thing," snapped her mother, holding the French letter at arm's length and hurrying over to the garbage-bin. A gang of pimply kids looked at her, then one another, and started cackling.

So hot. Who'd want to be cuddling anyone this weather? Deirdre Kincaid thought with longing of the cold airs at the other side of the world, rain blowing in cold and sleety, days of rain, with cool air to be breathed in.

It was a drought, everyone said. What sort of a country is it that gives you floods one summer and drought the next. Much more of this and we'll wither up, all of us. She longed to feel the cold wind blowing her hair back. And most of all she longed to be away from the noise of jangling and grinding and squealing, some place where it was still, and the only sound was wings whirring overhead, and maybe not even that.

12

In the end, if you wait long enough, you get your wish. Maybe it doesn't come in time, or just the way you want it, but in a sort of a way you do get it. The blistering heat kept on all through January. One weekend the fun park was jam-packed, the next it was empty. Holidays were finished. School was in. And it was February, and it was raining.

Reg, his nerves worn to a frazzle after the helter-skelter of the season, was more touchy than she'd ever seen him. Everything set him off, nothing pleased him. He was angry that Hugh hadn't turned up to help for a few days.

"What could he do, Reg? There's not enough work here now for the two of us." She was sharp, because she was missing Hugh herself. She'd seen him only from a distance since Christmas: the truth was, she'd avoided him, content just to glimpse him through the crowds. But the sun went away and so did he.

Everything made Reg snappy: Bob was lazy, Tim had too much to say. The merry-go-round wasn't worth a bumper. His piles were giving him hell again.

"Go and see about an operation, Reg. You said you might."

"Never trust those blokes again after what they did to me last go. No, I'll grin and bear it."

Grin was one thing he didn't do. He never stopped airing his grievances. "What's the use of money when you've got nothing you want to do with it." Nothing was any good.

One day she got sick of his moaning. "You need a holiday, Reg. Go and look up some of your old mates, why don't you? Just shove Rusty in the back and get going. Right now."

Reg beamed. "Will you come, Dee?"

"No chance. I know when I'm well off. You and that truck, you don't need a third party along."

"Well, I might just take your advice." All of a sudden he was eager. "I might get going now. Then I'll be home by the weekend. Put up in the country pubs, see what I can pick up along the way." He didn't want to waste a minute. "Close up if you feel like it, Dee. Go over on the ferry and do a bit of shopping. Have a look at the Opera House, all that. Get that lazy bugger of a Hugh over to help you." He couldn't wait to be gone, his thoughts were miles away from her, on the country roads he was already travelling. "Alright love, thanks for the suggestion. Give us a kiss and I'll be off."

Deirdre, left alone, sighed: it was wet enough and dismal enough already: with him gone it'd be the most God-forsaken dump in the world. Still if she went back to the flat, that'd be worse. Would I like to see a picture, she wondered. They say it's nothing but porn now, I'm not too shook on porn, never was. Wish I was more of a reader, it'd be a good day to get a book and hole up in bed and listen to the rain outside. But—I'm not a reader—and I'd go round the bend just staring at the four walls and listening to it pouring down. Well at least there's cleaning up if I want something to do. I'll tidy out the office and get Reggie's papers in order.

She gazed out at the rain sweeping steadily across the concrete. Everything grey, sky and sea and concrete. But last week it was all yellow. That's life, she thought, take it or leave it, it's all you'll get. She leaned on her elbows, for once allowing herself to mope. First your ears nearly split open with the noise, then there's nothing but the slap of the water and the rain swishing in.

The little car stopped with a jerk. It was—it had to be—Hugh's car. She felt the blood leave her head. She bent her head over the counter, pretending to shuffle the boxes into line. Between her lashes she saw him coming, sprinting almost, skidding to a stop. When she looked up he was standing before her, drops of water in his bright hair and trickling down his face.

"Hi, Deirdre," he greeted her. "What a day! What a week!

Coaching in the rain—" he shook his head—"there's got to be another way to earn a living."

"Do they still turn up?" She didn't look at him.

"The keen ones do."

"The serious swimmers," she said, remembering. It seemed ages ago since he'd said that.

"What?" He started to laugh. "Yeah, that's right. Where's dad?"

Deirdre shrugged. "Don't know. He took off about half an hour ago. He's been like an old bear all week."

"He's been overdoing it. Still, it was a good summer. Bet he cleaned up." His face was greedy. Against her will she remembered what Jacky Mobbs had said about the scorpion in Hugh's pocket. But Jacky, he'd say anything. "More money in an amusement park than teaching swimming," he added thoughtfully.

"More dirt too." She kept on pretending to be busy, not looking at him, frightened he'd go, frightened he'd stay. Stupid, what was there to be frightened of?

"What's he gone to get this time?"

Deirdre shrugged. "Who knows? Last time it was a pianola he brought back, this time it might be a hippopotamus." She wished she could think of something clever to say. When she tried to be funny it came out sounding stupid, like that about the hippopotamus. What made her say hippopotamus?

But Hugh was grinning, rocking back and forth on his heels, saying it over to himself. "Hippopotamus. That's pretty good. He's a funny old guy alright. When's he coming back?"

Deirdre turned her palms upward, and with an effort looked into his face, the clear eyes, more grey than blue today. She could see the pulse in his throat beating. "Maybe the weekend, maybe not. Why?"

Hugh's face fell and he bit his bottom lip, it was a trick he had, she'd noticed it before. "I had something to tell him, that's all."

"Isn't it meant for my ears?"

"For both of you. He won't be back at all tonight then?"

Deirdre felt her temper rising as he kept on at it. A stubborn little bugger, Reg said, never knew when to let go. Well, she could be stubborn too. She turned her back on him, let him keep his secrets.

"I don't know, I told you. D'you want it in writing?" Let him treat her like an outsider, she'd do the same back again.

"Deirdre," said his voice, warm now and coaxing. "Turn round. Don't be sulky."

"I'm not sulky," she cried and swung round. For the first time since she'd known him she looked deep into his eyes, her lips parting in a smile.

"Well, get ready." He leaned towards her and she felt his warm breath. "Here we go. You're going to be a grandma."

Deirdre flinched as if he'd struck her. Her eyes ranged over his face, his throat and, at last, his body and his long legs. She put her hands under the counter to still their trembling. She could not get her breath. Her voice, when she was able to speak, sounded hollow and faraway.

"Where's your wife?" she heard herself ask.

"She's gone to Jindabyne to see her mother and tell her the good news." He moved one of the glass jars closer and screwed off the top, reaching in his long fingers with the gold hair across the knuckles. She watched while he took out two jelly snakes and held them up by the tails.

"Oh, the fat one," Deirdre heard herself say. "And doubtless she'll be monstrous too before it's all over."

Hugh looked puzzled. He ate the first snake slowly, starting with the tail; then he began to frown. She saw his Adam's apple move as he swallowed, and she breathed in the scent of fresh skin and soap and chlorine and chocolate that belonged to him and no one else. She stood waiting, willing herself not to cry out.

Hugh was frowning at her. "She'll be alright. I'll put her on a diet," he said. Then he blurted out what was puzzling him. "I must say you don't seem very pleased, Deirdre. I thought you'd be tickled pink."

Under the counter she dug her nails into her palms. She gave a laugh that meant nothing, so false and tinkly. All she wanted now was to have him gone. Go, please go, she said inside herself, over and over, willing him to leave. Aloud she cried, "Well I'm not your blood, am I, Hugh? Your father's the one who'll be singing the high notes." She felt herself shaking. "Do you think you could have a look at the merry-go-round? It keeps lurching, your father said."

"Takes after him," Hugh muttered.

She was glad to have the chance to be fierce, to be able to raise her voice before she burst with the effort of keeping it low. "Do you grudge him a bit of a drink? Should he be always sucking up cocoa like you?"

"You're funny today, Deirdre. What's got into you?"

"Nothing's got into me!" she almost yelled.

He was crestfallen. His face was glum, she was glad of it, she wished she could smack it; that's what she wanted to do, to hurt him.

"Gee, I thought you'd be pleased. I'm certainly glad that Sheila's not here. She'd be really hurt."

At the sound of that name Deirdre flared. Hurt, who cares if she's hurt. She wouldn't know how to be hurt anyway, as long as she's got her glad rags and the money for a bit of fun, as she calls it. She leaned forward, lashing out. "Who cares? It'd take more than that to hurt her. She's got a hide like a rhinoceros."

Hugh's mouth flew open. He moved back then forward, scowling into her face.

"Deirdre, what's up with you? You look—gosh, you look as if you're going to burst. What's wrong? Are you sick?" His face cleared. "You've had it. You've run yourself into the ground. I've seen swimmers do the same thing to themselves after a hard season. You've been knocking yourself out ever since Christmas."

"I haven't!" she cried. "It's not that. I haven't!"

"Take it easy." He patted her shoulder, trying to soothe her. She pulled away, but he kept on. "Day and night, well who could keep that up? Look, you close up now, it's dead as a doornail in here anyway. You get a good night's sleep and you'll feel a different person. I'll have a word with dad and tell him he's got to take better care of you. It's just overwork, that's all. You're thin as—gee, you're far too thin, Deirdre."

She gave in. The alarm on his face was balm to her, and the soft note in his voice.

"I will then, I'll take your advice. I'll go now. Would you like to come up for a cup of cocoa? I'll make you one."

He hesitated, then shook his head. "Better not. By the time I find out what's wrong and get it fixed—" He glanced at his watch. "You know dad. If he asks you to do something he wants it done on the spot."

"Later on, then?"

"I've got to go to a coaches' meeting," he answered. "Worse luck."

But whether he really thought it was worse luck or not she couldn't tell. She gave a great sigh, and looked past him at the clowns, their empty faces, their open mouths.

Alone in the flat she looked for work and found none. She felt more tired than she'd ever felt, yet she knew that sleep wouldn't come for the asking. If she went to the chemist, maybe he'd give her something. Or maybe Reg had some sleeping-tablets. In the little medicine box she found a bottle full of pain-killers, and in another bottle, one sleeping tablet, just one. What I really need is something strong enough to knock me out forever, she thought. But once before I felt like this, and I lived on, and in the end I got over it. But then what did I live on for? For years to be dozing, then to wake up to this, what I can't keep from myself any longer: this aching for a boy that can never be mine. So what is there in life, then? Reg, he's got his work and his boy and now his grandchild. At the thought of the child and all that went along with it, she threw herself on her bed, shaking with rage and with jealousy. So she'd have Hugh now, that girl, and the child as well. Somehow I missed the way, it could have been mine, all of it, if I hadn't thrown all those years down the drain. But the sign I was waiting for, it never came, not till now. Is this what you call being alive, then? This terrible feeling of being tossed around like a fishing-boat in a tempest? That's what he meant about my mother, the priest: poor child, he said, she was the plaything of the elements, I thought he said elephants, it made no sense to me. Let me go back to being a zombie, then. Not to feel anything, it's better than this, anything's better than this—Yet there was something, his voice was tender when he spoke to me. Maybe she'll die having the baby, or get run over, or run off with someone and leave the baby behind. Is it the baby I want then, that my heart's jumping up at the thought. I don't know what I want.

She started to sob, racking sobs that hurt her throat. It was years since she'd cried. Now she gave herself up to it and sobbed till her head was throbbing and her eyeballs felt on fire. She lay on the bed, shivering. At last she pulled off her clothes and crawled between the sheets and lay there, staring up into the darkness, waiting for sleep to come and set her free.

And she slept. Sleeping, she dreamed. She was back in Ireland, running, always running, trying to catch something always out of her reach, the ground was stony and she kept stumbling, she'd come to the end of the road, she was standing still. In front of her was a wall of fire, there against the wall, with his back to her, was a man in dark clothes, she heard herself cry out to him and he turned, swinging violently round. Sprawled in his arms was a child, the man was laughing at her and his mouth framed a word, Catch, and the child came hurtling towards her. She tried to run to catch him, her feet stuck fast, she tried to scream—

Deirdre woke screaming, the sound of her scream bouncing

back from the walls. Where?—She was where?—It seemed forever till she knew herself in her bedroom, in her bed, at the other side of the world. But what she felt in the dream was still happening. Her breathing came in gasps. She put her hands up to her cheeks and took them away, wet. She heard the rain beating down. With great weariness she got up and moved to the window; and she stood there, looking out at the slice of dark water.

If I see this through, and there's nothing good comes out of it, then I'll set out again and find some place I can be peaceful and maybe some man who'll love me and a child who'll be mine. And signs, no, there'll be no more waiting for signs. I'll be done with signs and waiting. But first I'll see it through.

13

Easter is the tail-end of the summer season. Fun parks and surfing and swimming have had their day, and the football matches, that's where they go to eat and yell. Just before the end there's one last burst. It's the Easter show that cuts the year right down the middle. The kids from the country come over for the ferry-ride and sometimes men with broad-brimmed hats. And the crowd from the city comes pushing over for one last fling; after that it's the off season and they only come in a trickle.

Easter crowds are different from the ones that come at Christmas. They move like people at the end of a holiday, not the start. Their summer clothes are a bit raggy and their tans are starting to fade. There's not so much flirting or fighting going on, and they don't push as hard to get their food or their tickets. It's as if the winter that's coming has got into their bones. For all their skylarking they're just whistling in the dark.

Like me, mused Deirdre. Going through the motions, that's all. Putting in time to see what the winter brings, and if spring's going to be any better. Waiting round. Looking up all the time to catch a glimpse of someone I don't want to see, and he never comes here anyway. Scared out of my wits in case the goldy head in the crowd turns out to be his.

It was afternoon. The holiday-makers were coming back from the show, weighed down with sample bags and toy monkeys and windmills. Children were cranky, giving cheek, kicking out at one another. Mothers were fagged-out. Fathers were walking ahead, not looking back. Deirdre, busy, but not flat-out, glanced up automatically as each ferry tipped them out on to the quay. Sometimes a few kids found they had money left in their pockets and came across to spend it. A few headed for the ocean, trying to get in another swim before the tides turned cold.

The four o'clock ferry came in. The gangplank was lowered. Deirdre glanced up from the kiosk, across the wide concrete strip that separated the fun park from the wharf. The ferry had pulled in at the western side today.

And she saw Hugh coming down the gangplank, tall and brown, with a Mexican hat on the back of his head, sample bags over one arm. And his other arm over the shoulder of a girl in a blue smock: Sheila, fatter, and her hair streaming loose. She was giggling, her head thrown back; in one hand she was holding a fat-bellied kewpie on a stick.

As Deirdre watched, they turned to each other, their steps slowing, and the crowd swallowed them up.

14

It was strange, that long hot summer that ended in rain, with the sun back at Easter, shining down hot, but not scorching. Then rain again, that never let up, not even for a day, the sleety icy sort of rain you knew would go on forever if it had a mind to. All May it rained, all June, and kept it up as July came in. The wettest period in history, said the weather man, and likely to get worse.

Hugh had disappeared, taking Sheila with him. They'd given up the flat and hired a caravan to go sight-seeing round New South Wales. Since the day he'd told her about the baby he had never put in an appearance at the park. But Reg was in touch with him and had all the news at his finger-tips. Reg was overcome with joy, you'd think nobody had ever been a grandfather before: just the prospect of it took ten years off his age. He was bubbling with schemes, he was going to settle half the season's takings on the nipper, take out insurance for him, put his name down for King's School. Every week he added another plan to the list. It'd be a boy, no way not. The Kincaids, they all have boys, that's why the name keeps going. He rubbed his hands together with glee whenever he spoke of the future, which was often.

Deirdre moved through the shortening days, quiet but alive and watchful, biding her time. If anyone had asked her what she was waiting for she couldn't have answered. Something would happen soon, she was certain. She went on little excursions with Reg, driving through the rain up to the Blue Mountains, to see the autumn leaves; but instead of red and gold they were brown and slushy, lying on the ground, rotting. The frosts hadn't come to colour them, only the rain to make them sodden. Once they drove to Kurrajong to hear the bell-birds, but that was the day they didn't choose to sing.

"How'd you get to be so docile, Dee?" Reg asked her.

Whatever his suggestion was, she was ready to fall in with it. And they came thick and fast, those suggestions of his. Want to see the reptile park, Dee? How about a little run up to Palm Beach? Tell you what, it might be an idea if we go down Kiama way, let you have a look at the blowhole.

"If you like, Reg," she said each time.

The only thing she insisted on, she had to be back home at night. Why, she didn't know. But wherever his whim took them, the three of them, counting Rusty in the back, she made no complaint.

So he was happy, Reg, in spite of the rain, he said he'd never got enough of her company before. Not that she could see what he got out of it, to have her sitting there by his side, while he talked on and on about the roads he'd travelled and the narrow escapes he'd had from every kind of peril you could name. Every story he told reminded him of another one. Just as well she wasn't one to babble.

At weekends they opened the fun park to pitiful business. Reg stood Bob down first, then Tim. In spring, he said they'd be more than welcome to come back; if he paid them now he'd be running at a loss.

But it would never be spring. The rain would never stop.

One wet Sunday night they sat over tea, Reg spouting. He finished his cup of tea and pushed back his chair.

"Let's see what's on telly."

"Might as well get rid of this first." She stood up and began to clear away the dishes. To sit still, it took too much out of her.

"Leave them love. I'll take them out in a minute and do them. Come over and sit here next to me. I want to try a little bit of friendly persuasion."

"Oh, I might as well get it out of the way." She moved restlessly. "This rain's never going to stop."

"Lucky we didn't get it at Christmas." Reg opened the

newspaper in case he'd missed something in the morning. "We'd have gone broke. There's such a thing as too much rain." She didn't answer. "If it keeps on going we'll need an ark. Deirdre, how about coming up north when I go. You'd like it. It'll put the roses back in your cheeks. We'll keep going till we leave the rain behind us."

She dumped the plates in the sink and came back for the casserole. Why she didn't want to go she couldn't say. There was nothing to keep her here. And she'd be lonely all by herself, she hated the thought of that, all that loose time to fill in. But she knew she had to stay.

"You go, Reg. If you're going on business you won't want me round anyway."

"Well, that's one of the things I wanted to talk to you about. Looks like we'll be renewing the lease next year. I got wind of that merry-go-round, you know the one I was telling you about, I hear it's up for sale again. I've got to do something about that bomb we've got, it won't last another season. I had a talk to Dooley, he said he's prepared to sell it and let us install our own. Long as we give him first offer if we go. That seem fair to you? He knows it's nothing but trouble, he said as much."

"Who'd buy it then?"

"Oh it's a light job. Easy to dismantle. A travelling show, it'd suit them down to the ground." Reg shot her a glance. "Dooley said he'd sell it to me if I like, then I can get rid of it whenever I want to. He's too old to be bothered mucking about."

"So we're going to have two of them? Look Reg, I don't care, you'll do whatever you want anyway."

"Well it's your money too. You worked for it." No doubt he looked well, his eyes bright, not bloodshot these days because he was off the grog. "But if I could get hold of this one we'd make our fortune. You've never seen anything like it in your life, Dee. Dragons and gilded lions as well as the swans and horses—and those what d'you call 'em—black-uh—blackamoors."

"It'd be too fancy for a place like this Reg," she said,

indifferently. "But I don't know why I'm talking, you'll have your own way. No wonder you've never got any money."

He took no notice. "We can make room for it if we just shuffle things round a bit, get rid of some of the junk. That's the other thing I wanted to say—how about getting rid of the waxworks? They're not worth a cracker. It's a fair-sized room. We could fix it up for the kids to live in for three or four months, rig up a shower, well it wouldn't be any worse than what they've got. It'd save them a bit of money while Hugh's laid off." She swivelled round. "Well don't look like that, what did I say wrong?—You could get it fixed up while I was away. Give you something to do."

"No." Her voice was icy.

Reggie sighed. "Well, what *would* make you happy then? Oh come on Dee, a trip'll do you good. It's a waste of time opening this weather. If we get away now we'll be home in plenty of time for the baby."

She couldn't speak for the pain she felt.

"You'll like it better when the baby's born." He sighed. "You should have a baby of your own, that's half the trouble." He stopped, then hurried on. "Alright, alright, I take it back. But I tell you this Dee, I can hardly wait. I'll never forget when Hughie was a little bloke.—Well if you won't come I'll get Tim to look in on you." He looked at her face. "God Almighty, Dee, what can I do to make you happy? Will I take you back to Ireland then? Forget the bloody hurdy-gurdy?"

"Why? There's nothing for me there." She picked up the tray and went out to the sink.

15

So he'd gone. And he'd be back in a while. He shilly-shallied for a month, then he got going. And today was her first day of waiting and being alone, and already she was wondering why she'd bothered to stay, and how she'd get through the rest of the week with the torment in her head, she didn't dare to think.

"So I want him, then, Hugh, whatever the cost," she said aloud, blindly staring down at the sock she was holding in her clenched fist. Alright then, that's how it is: it's a fellow that I've got no right to. I'll take it all out and I'll look it straight in the eye and maybe then it won't seem like a nest of devils. He's Reggie's boy, and Reggie loves me and he doesn't. And Reggie's worth a dozen of him and he hardly knows I'm alive. And he's head over turkey wrapped up in that thing he's married to, that turns it on for him morning and night and noontimes too, by the look of her.   Deirdre shook all over at the picture of the two of them together: she knew what he'd be like, so quick and clean and greedy, like a boy. And the way he'd cry out, she knew that too. I know him like the back of my hand.

She looked down at her hand; she'd pulled it off her fist with the needle still in it, that sock she was darning. There was a long scratch, bleeding. Yet for all that I'll go to my grave without knowing him, unless—Unless what? Unless something—

On the stairs outside there came a clattering. Somebody was leaping up, two stairs at a time, Tim it'd be. It was Tim?—

It was Hugh. His fresh deep voice called from the doorway, no not to her, but to his father.

"Paper!" he was calling out. "Read all about it. You there, dad?" As he finished calling he came inside. "Oh it's you, Deirdre." He halted.

Since summer's end he'd grown a beard, springy and thick and reddish. If he was handsome before, then what would you call him now, with the boy's smile behind the beard that made him look a man? He stood next to the mirror, not seeing it, and was reflected a dozen times over.

"So it's you," Deirdre said at last. "It's a long time since I set eyes on you." She looked at his reflection, whole in the centre panel of the glass, splintered in the panels around. "And now there's a hundred of you. Like a hundred princes."

He moved and all the young men in the mirror followed him. His voice was gruff. "What are you talking about princes for? Doesn't make sense to me. Where's dad?"

Deirdre Kincaid was calm, icy in the head for all the tingling in her fingers and the heaviness in her thighs. She smiled at him, coaxing him to smile back, and at last he did.

"He's still chasing that hurdy-gurdy. It's like the bunyip, he keeps hearing news of it."

"You've got to be kidding." He pulled over a chair and straddled it. Seeing her calm and easy he was calm too.

Deirdre shook her head. "No I'm not. He won't rest till he gets his hands on it." Her words sounded in her ears like someone reciting.

"Why didn't you go with him? He told me you'd been doing a lot of travelling."

"So have you. And now you're back."

He shifted uncomfortably. "Yeah. Well, we got too much rain along the way. The caravan leaked. It's not the most comfortable way of moving about."

"I got tired of travelling too."

The summer's gold was fading from his hair, but his eyes' bright stare was still the same, and the feeling of energy he brought into any room with him. That's being young, she thought, young and healthy. It only comes for a while in your life, and when it's gone it's gone forever. It's when you've never had a real backhander, and you think you can get anything you want, if only you want it hard enough.

"Dad's stupid to spend that kind of money. He'll never get any return for it." He stood up, ready to go. The shoulders of his cardigan were damp with rain. "Well, I won't hang around."

Something, she had to say something to keep him. Her eyes fell on the paper under his arm. "What's in the paper?"

He shrugged. "Nothing, really, it's always the same old stuff. Another young girl murdered. Two banks robbed. Just the same. They're at it again in Ireland."

"Not again. Still," said Deirdre, standing now and moving towards him, taking the paper he held out as if to keep her off. "That's why I left it for good and all." She opened the paper, pretending to read; and stared down at the face that stared up at her.

That face. From the other side of the world he'd come now to haunt her, as once he'd come to haunt her dreams. Her hands shook. The paper fell to the ground.

"Is it Dermond O'Neill? I can't see. Did they kill him?" she whispered.

Hugh bent to pick the paper up. In silence he looked at the printed page.

"Yes," he told her. "Oh no, wait a sec—he killed himself so's he wouldn't be captured. He's the one they've been after."

Her head swam. She almost fell.

Hugh put his arms around her, pulled her close to his warm body. "What's wrong? Are you sick? Deirdre—are you alright now?"

She swayed against him, her mind in a whirl. Her mouth pressed against the wool of his jacket and he held her tight to stop her from falling and it seemed that it was Dermond who held her. So she'd never see him again, never, and that was the end of it then. She saw him again as he cried to her to stay, not to leave him, how he caught her hand to pull her back and she cried to God to punish him. And now he was dead. She gave a cry that was almost a howl. The moment he died it's likely I was sleeping, or mooning after a boy. And now it's too late, and what's done can't be undone. And if I hate him or love him I don't know, but I don't want him dead. She sagged against

Hugh.

"Deirdre. You'd better lie down. Look, let me—" He tightened his grasp around her body. Half-leading, half-pushing, he guided her towards the bedroom. There was no power in her legs, as if she no longer owned them.

She fell across her bed and lay still, staring up at the ceiling. Then she jerked up, half-leaning against the pillow, her face turned to him. With an effort she spoke.

"He was my husband. He still is. I had no right to marry your father."

He was shocked, so his face said to her. He waited, swallowing, for her to go on.

All the torment she'd buried all those years back, all that she'd pushed behind her and refused to look at, it rose now to her lips. As she spoke she saw it all as she'd seen it the day her life ended.

"He was tampering with fireworks to the end then," she said with all the bitterness stored up in her. "He killed our little boy."

It was all there before her, clear as the day it happened: the green turf before the white house, and the baby running barefoot, his feet sinking into the grass, and the red of his hair shining in the sunlight. "Mumma," he was calling, "Mumma," chirping like a little bird as he ran into her arms. Dermond with the great crock he was filling, his mouth stern, the dimple in his chin deep as a valley. And under the table the box of grenades that he'd promised her he'd take back . . . What was he doing with the gunpowder, then? Best you don't know, he'd said when she asked. He was pouring it into the crock. When he heard Neilly he looked up laughing, and he left the crock on the table, and the box, and he came over to squeeze them both in his arms. But Neilly kicked and wriggled till he got free; and Dermond, he turned her face to his, and kissed her lips, and pressed his legs against her, and unbuttoned her blouse—

And the noise—   It was everywhere   And everywhere it was red   and his blood, it hit her in the face and blinded her. She clawed it away and   what she saw

She opened her eyes and looked at the boy's face near hers, so like Neilly, so like it was uncanny. And she remembered it then, yes, that was why she'd come to love him, because he looked like her little boy.

"He didn't mean to?" asked Hugh, very low.

"Oh no. My little boy, he—They think he got a grenade—It exploded—I had to forget it or I couldn't go on living.—But I didn't go on living!" she cried out. "It was the end of my life." Her voice was quite flat. "All the life drained out of me and it left me no more than a ghost. For years I dreamed it over and over again. I ran away from the dream but it followed me all over the world. I used to wake up screaming. Then the dreams stopped and I knew that I was dead. He would have been like you, my little boy, strong like you and beautiful. When I saw you I felt as if he'd been given back to me. That night in the waxworks—I can't tell you how I felt—If I could only make you know. I felt my blood stir and my heart began to beat again. I—" She fought for words to make him see. "When you stood there with your lips parted, it was Neilly grown up." She began to put out her hands to Hugh, sitting still as a stone on the end of the bed, saying nothing, not a word. She sat straight up. "Can you imagine what it's like to be brought back to life?"

He moved uneasily. "I don't know what to say. I've never heard a story like that.—Gosh you've got yourself in a state, Deirdre."

For answer she seized his hand and kissed it.

He pulled it away. He turned his face from her. "I'm not your son, Deirdre. Look, I know you've had a tough trot, but—" His whole body was rigid with fear—was it fear? "I'm out of my depth. Look, don't put me up on a pedestal. I'm just not your son, that's all." He stood up.

Deirdre rose from the bed to face him, quite beside herself. She looked full into his face, not hiding her love for him. She looked into those eyes that would never meet hers in love, that shifted away now in panic. With a tremendous effort of will she got hold of herself.

"I know you're not. But I think the world of you." Her skin was as tight as a mask, her voice was a sing-song. "You'll come and tell me when the baby's born, won't you?"

Hugh was grinning, at his ease now, and happy. "Actually, that's what I came to tell dad, you and dad, I mean. The doctor's putting her into hospital tonight. She's a week overdue, they say now, but she reckons it's a fortnight. Anyway they reckon they've got to get things moving. She's in great shape, never stopped doing her exercises. Looks as if I'll have good news for you this time tomorrow."

Deirdre Kincaid held out her hands. "Soon as that?" she asked, and her lips curved back in the ghost of a smile.

"I'd better be going," he told her. "I've got to get Sheila over to the hospital. She had a bit of last minute packing to do." At the door he looked down at the paper that had fallen to the carpet. He picked it up and folded it over. "Sorry about all that, Deirdre," he muttered.

She did not answer.

Out on the balcony, where she'd hastened to see him leaving, thinking maybe she'd call him back, make him know how she felt—out where she'd stood, silent, calling out nothing because there was no way she could reach him—out there on the balcony she waited while the hours passed. She saw the sun drop down behind the western hills, and the homecomers streaming out, making for the places they belonged. She saw the lights snap on, along the pier, and the dark hulk of the fun park. She heard the din of the traffic and sometimes the slapping of the water and the little birds settling into sleep. But she saw nothing and she heard nothing as she stood and sat and stood again and, in the end, lay down on the lumpy day-bed, shivering in the night air, staring up into the dark. She thought of the girl Sheila, and the baby on its way into the world, and she started to cry, remembering her own baby butting his way out, first the horrible grinding pains then the end of it, when you thought you were being torn apart, all your insides leaving you. Then they put him in your arms and nothing in the world ever equalled that moment.—And she thought there's no way I can stand any more, I'll have to be done with it all now. But if I can't have him, Hugh, there's no way I'll leave him for anyone else.

And as soon as she knew that she was quite calm and she stretched out, composed, and pushed her head down into the cushion; and she went to sleep.

She was walking barefoot along a beach, looking for something that was never there, it was a place she'd never seen before, with stones rolling over her feet and tripping her, her feet were bleeding, still she kept pushing on, against a black wind, till she came to the thing that was waiting for her. It looked like a box but she knew it was a coffin. She knelt down because this was what she had to do, feeling for the catch with stiff fingers. At first it resisted and then it sprang open with a click. She started away from it and when she looked down it was—of course it was the headless woman, blood on her waxen dress and on one of her fingers the ring from the fair.

It changed then and she was walking in her sleep along the boardwalk beside the old pool, in the dusk, no lights anywhere, only the gleam of the water both sides of the torn netting. She leaned over and saw her face mirrored in water, with huge eyes, dark and huge as wells. Behind her, close to her ears, a voice sprang out at her, "If you want to jump try the other side It's deeper."

16

In the morning, moving heavily, stepping over the worn brown lino in the kitchen too small for her, she went about the task she had to do. She took out two cups and two saucers, the big breakfast cups with the willow pattern that Hugh said he liked, big enough, he said, for a man to quench his thirst.

She took down cocoa and sugar, and mixed them carefully in each cup, more cocoa than usual. Then she went to the cupboard where it was stored away, the plastic bucket stacked with the boxes that they'd brought back from the fun park, with Poison painted on the lid in big red letters, with the paint left over from the clowns' noses.

So this is the end of it all for both of us, she thought, and she saw, like something behind veils, Reggie's face, with his son gone and his wife into the bargain. "There's nothing to be done," she said aloud, without anger or pity. If I can't have him one way then it's got to be the other. I didn't ask for it to happen, any of it. And the image of her little son and her son grown up to manhood and her young husband who did the killing and set it all going, they all ran together in her mind, and which was which she couldn't tell. We're all bound the same way so the sooner we get on with it the better: there's no time to waste getting it all behind me.

She took out the top carton and read the directions. How big is a rat compared to a person, a hundred rats, do they make up one man? I've got to be sure to put in enough for both of us, to do the job right. Tasteless, he said, and odourless. Great stuff, he said. She remembered his face that day, and she faltered. Back from his honeymoon, she remembered, and grew hard. Now he'll have a chance to try his own medicine.

She took what she needed, then a bit more. It's like making tea, one for each person and one more for the pot. I'm doing him a good turn, he'll never know what it is to be old and sick, or have the girls turn away from him, those that look at him all the time now with sweet eyes. He'll never know what it is to puff and pant like his father, and see his legs grow skinny while his belly grows big. And I'll hold him in my arms at last, and whatever there is in store, we'll find it together. She sealed up the packet, replaced it, jammed down the lid, put the bucket in its place and shut the cupboard door.

Then she mixed it in, half to each cup. She put a saucer on top of each, to keep the flies away, even in winter they came to pester her. Pests, I'll be done with all of them, and those headaches that haven't left me for months. Not sleeping, I'll be done with that too. Life, if you haven't the one thing that makes it worthwhile, it's not worth the torment.

She filled the kettle and put it on a low flame. Then she went to wash her hands. Soon he would come. All I have to do now is wait. She combed her hair and reddened her lips. Her face was dead white, even the freckles faded away. I'll never look at that face again, she thought, that's funny to think of.

She moved her purple chair so that she could see the door, and sat down to wait. He wouldn't be long coming, she knew that. How do I know, she asked herself, maybe it'll take days. No, it'll be soon, this morning. She picked up her knitting, a long scarf she'd taken a fancy to make, all the colours of the rainbow. It'll never get finished now, she thought, I'm glad of that, I was tired of it long ago. Funny when you make up your mind how little you care about anything you're leaving behind you. It's the journey in front that means everything, and making sure you don't bungle the last of the preparations.

Come soon, darling, she willed him, light-headed she felt from lack of sleep. How long since I've slept? Days it must be since I've had a proper sleep. And since I've eaten, days and days. She picked up the knitting that had fallen from her hands and began to knit. By the time I've finished this row he'll be here, with the news spilling out of his lips. How did she know then? That girl would take no time with the job, so young and healthy. It was like that for me. That terrible last push, then they put the baby on my belly, and I lifted myself up to see him. She remembered the feel of the little mouth at her breast. And the first smile he gave that wasn't wind, and the first time his hands reached out, his eyes crossing and his neck wobbling with the effort. And his first steps, staggering, and how he tried to say mumma, bubbling it out. All the things she'd never let herself remember came crowding into her mind, one picture pushing another out. And when she thought of Reggie she hardened her heart. He'll have the young one to bring up, she'll let him in on the job. I can't help the way it turned out. It's just that I can't have my boy living in the world and lying in another woman's arms. Reggie, he'll have to do the best he can.

The row was done. She put it from her, over on the table, and she waited for what she knew would happen, that the one she wanted would come racing up the stairs to her.

And he came. And the voice she loved above any in the world, it called her name.

"Deirdre. You there Deirdre?"

He sounded warm and happy, and full of tenderness for her. She stood up, light in the head, and crossed to the door, and opened it to him. There he stood, beaming all over his face, that lovely face of his that she longed to hold between her hands. Be still, she warned herself, wait, your turn will come.

"It's a boy." His voice was loud with excitement, as loud as a schoolboy's.

"A boy," she breathed, leaning towards him, making her lips move in a smile as wide as his. "That's what you wanted."

"I knew we'd have a boy. Wait till dad hears."

From her distance, she felt glad: so Reggie would have that left, his son to bring up again, starting from the very start. In the end we all got what was fair.

"That's wonderful," she heard a soft voice say, her own voice. "Is Sheila well?"

He was walking around the room, not able to settle, sitting

then getting up. "A hundred per cent. You know Sheila."

"Yes, I know," said that soft sing-song voice. "Tell me about it."

He sat down on the sofa, then he jumped up. His hair was roughed-up and his shirt rumpled, she had never seen him so upside-down and full of life. "I'm too excited to sit still. We'll have to celebrate. Wait till you see him. He's a beauty!"

"I suppose you haven't eaten all day?" She looked at his hands, as he punched one into the other, the scar shaped like a half-moon, above the wedding-ring she'd never been able to look at. But now it was alright to look, she felt no jealousy. She gazed into his eyes, looking deep, not glancing away.

"Look at you," she said, teasing him—or maybe it was the girl she'd once been that was speaking. "I've never seen you so merry.—Have you eaten?"

He shook his head. "Too excited to eat. He's a whopper. Nearly nine pounds. Twenty two inches long. Wait till dad sees him. He'll have him winning the Olympics, year two thousand." He crossed his arms, laughing.

Deirdre stood up. "I'll make you a cup of cocoa. Sit there and calm yourself down, if you can. I'll only be a moment."

The kettle was bubbling quietly on the gas jet. It was only a moment to bring it to the boil. She poured the water into the cups, stirred it in, and added milk, and on the top she floated the cream that he liked. She picked up the tray and carried it through the doorway. The long glass caught and held him, whole, then in little pieces, broken up.

"What will you call him?" she asked, handing him his cup.

"We haven't decided yet. Sheila likes Damien. But I think it's a bit too fancy. Got to think about school, if he'll get stirred with a name like that.—Oh gee—"

She watched while he lifted the cup to his lips, almost drank, then set it back in the saucer. "I'm too excited to drink."

Deirdre smiled to see his joy: that's the time to leave the party, when it's all joy.

"Drink it up," she murmured. "And I'll have mine. It'll do us both good."

He took his cup again, holding it between his two hands. Then he took a great swig, as she knew he would, the way he always downed his drink. He gagged. "It tastes—It—"

He put it on the floor and got to his feet, half retching, clutching at his belly, his eyes turning up, while she stood watching.

Noise broke the silence between them. Someone was clattering up the stairway, hammering on the door. She took no notice, but stood motionless. Soon it would be over, only a moment now.

"Deirdre, you there Deirdre? Any news yet? Thought I saw—"

"I can't—" Hugh was croaking. Then his voice was loud, swelling out loud. "She's poisoned me," he called. And through the door they'd left on the latch Tim came bursting.

"I'm poisoned!" He flung out his hand, his arm flailing, catching her cup, overturning it, knocking it to the floor, stumbling against his own cup.

Still in her dream, yet moving swiftly, Deirdre bent to salvage what she could. But the cups were empty. She fell to her knees, trying to scoop up what she could. But it had spread into a puddle over the carpet, there was only enough to wet her hands.

"I can't," she sobbed. "I can't, I can't—" She fell forward and lay there, not making a sound, at the end of her tether, her face pressed into the gritty carpet, her eyes shut tight.

17

Now they had her in their power at last, all those she'd feared, all those long years, the ones who say what's to be done with you, and deal it out to you, the way they'd dealt it out before. First they'd given her all in life she craved for, then they took it away.

Now they had her. First they put her in a cell, and then in a court-room, then back in a cell again. And they tried first to make her see the one she never wanted to set eyes on, the old fellow who loved her, whose heart she'd near broken. And when she cried out no, she wouldn't, they sent a young lawyer to help her get out of it, to tell her what to say, how she was half-starved and run-down, and it was just the moment's madness. But she wouldn't talk to him, she hardly opened her lips, only to say she didn't want to be let off.

"Who wants to be free?" she said to him. He was the mad one, trying to get her off. "Free," she said. "I can't ever be free."

Then he went away. But he told her before he went that Hugh was alive, not dead, and ready to forgive her because she was out of her mind.

"Get out," she said. So he went away, muttering it was on her own head.

"I can't help you, Mrs Kincaid, if you won't save yourself."

"That's good," she said. "Now stay away."

The women in the gaol they left her alone. She ate little and she drank little and she kept to herself. It was all over bar shouting, as Reg used to say.

In the end they took her into the court-room to answer the charges. When she saw Hugh there, with lines in his forehead and his thatch of hair thinned out, she wondered why she had tried to kill him, yes, she thought, I must have been mad. She tried to turn away, but the policewoman pushed her on. And Reggie there, sitting with Hugh, bony in the face, staring straight ahead. Took that to make Reggie thin, she thought in surprise, and she wanted to call out and tell him how sorry she was that it turned out like that. But he'd be alright, he'd suffered worse blows, or close on, he'll bounce back again the way he always does. Maybe though he thinks he's got to have me around and look after me. But he'll get over it when I'm out of the way.

She stood silent while they took turns talking and firing questions. And the fellow who was supposed to get her off, in a way he did what he thought best, talking about the explosion, and Dermond—Hugh must have told him—all of it. It didn't upset her to have it told, it seemed like someone else's story. And the Q.C. as they called him, the one they'd brought to tear her to bits, he got a lot of pleasure from his turn. It was all like a dream, like those dreams that were the start of it all—and what was dream now and what was real she couldn't rightly say.

She stood alone, only answering when they kept on at her, and then only in a word. She saw the faces of the reporters, getting it down for the papers, for people to read all about it, like they did about my baby, and like Dermond, anything for a thrill. She saw all the people done up for an outing, not missing a word, and the ones that ran the court, all of them, all doing their act. And she knew then that this was what was in store for her, what she'd been sent to the other end of the world to find: it was the last of her punishment, for not watching over her boy, so she could be tortured, and offered him again then have him snatched away.

"Answer the question, if you please, madam," he was saying, turning on her his face like a skull. "Or once again have you nothing to say?"

When she turned her head away from him she caught sight of Reggie's face, crumpled up, and she murmured something under her breath.

"Louder, if you please. We all wish to be enlightened."

She heard a tired voice in the background, "I object Your Honour." That's what he'd been saying forever, over and over like the pianola.

She looked into the cruel face and she said it again. "Kill me and be done with it."

All over the court-room they were rustling and coughing. She thought she could hear a baby crying: maybe it was Sheila, and she'd brought the baby to rub salt in the wounds.

If a skull can laugh, then the skull with a wig on top was laughing at her. "That is hardly indicated. There is really no need for Irish histrionics, Mrs Kincaid. We're not going to kill you."

Deirdre Kincaid gave him his answer. Not that she cared all that much for the last word, but she remembered she was Irish then, and she should hold up her head for that one thing, as Dermond had.

She stood up straight, and she made her voice strong, and she looked him straight in the eye. "I've got no fear of dying. You'd be doing me a favour. I want to be dead."

At last they let her go. They talked at her, and sometimes they raged at her, and they brought everyone she'd ever known to stand up there and talk about her. But she listened to none of them, not to Hugh, not to Reggie. They all kept arguing or showing off or going through the rigmarole while she sat with her head turned away, waiting for it to be done.

And in the end they told her to go: she was free. She was mad, they said, temporarily of insane mind, that's how they put it. And now, it seemed, she wasn't mad any more. She didn't have to be locked up. They took her down the back stairs, away from the photographers—but one was there, anyway.

She melted into the crowds of people shopping. No one knew her, no one at all. The way the crowds walked, she walked too.

The lights changed, and she went with them. She found herself standing still before a shop with a sign Love Shop. A man closed in on her and pressed himself against her, whispering something.

She drew away and began to walk the other way, back up the hill. She crossed at the lights. Lovers in jeans went past her, walking close, holding hands. She came to the big old store, as big as a palace, that Reggie used to call the Rolls-Royce, but now it was all broken-down, dirty and decaying, nobody to run it the right way, just dozens of small shops sprouting out of it. She stood near a window full of wax dummies, made of hard pink stuff, with their arms out stiffly in front of them. She heard two Chinamen talking Chinese behind her, and she thought she knew what they were saying, if she tried just a bit harder she'd know. When a gang of teenage boys pushed her out of their way she let herself be pushed. This is how a leaf feels when the winds blow it, she thought, moving this way and that, at their will. When the shoulders bumped her she went walking across the road towards the park, and she remembered another park, standing with her mother, the leaves swirling about them, and her mother, with a woollen cap pulled down over her ears, crying, and the dry leaves crackling around their ankles. It was autumn then? And now it's spring? Is it spring? Or summer, maybe by now it's summer? Her mouth felt dry. She passed the white lacy chairs on the green, with friends sitting chatting by the pots of those flowers called—called petunias. She heard the soft whirring of the pigeons' wings as they came for their bread. The heat of the day still came up from the pavement. She felt detached from all of it, as if she was walking in her sleep. Where am I going, she wondered. She came to the great fountain, its jets spouting into the basin, with crusts of bread floating, as they'd floated near the jetty. Her head felt very light and very full at the same time. Soon it'll be night, she thought, that's good. The shadows were long, the people coming out of their offices in a stream all pouring out, making for home, all the young girls, pretty in their summer dresses, not a mark on their faces. They'll find out, she thought.

She crossed the road when the lights told her, and then again, against the lights. She moved on past the place that was a morgue, no, a hospital, and the big black pig with a ring in his snout. That was the Italian pig he was talking about, Reggie, how you had to scratch his back for luck, or maybe it was the snout you rubbed. He'd tried to save her, poor Reg, waste of time, it was all better left unsaid.

So now she was walking through the garden gates, down the steps with flowers blooming, past the boys and girls stretched out face to face on the lawn. A woman with a baby in a pram hurried past her, late going home, no doubt. She went down the stairs, past the statues, and there, not too far in front of her, across a stretch of grass, was the grey sea-wall. So she kept on until she was there, and put her arms on the wall, and leaned her head on her arms, while she thought, yes, I'll make an end to it now. But when she looked there were people watching her, so if she jumped there'd be one of them jumping in to pull her out again. She stayed quiet, listening to her own breathing. I haven't smelled grass for a long time, not since—she couldn't remember when. She saw the sun go down behind the buildings and the pink reflection in the east, bright pink first, then paler, then grey. The lights sprang out on the far shore.

"They'll be closing up soon," said a man, standing close to her. He had bare feet and his face kept twitching.

She moved away from him and began to hurry, but he came after her, first mumbling, then shouting, a stream of swear words spilling out of his mouth. But when some other stragglers caught them up he stopped, and they all passed through the gates together.

And now she was walking on the green bank above the pavement, down to the harbour in the deepening dark; she kept steadily on, across the road where the buses were coming thick, squeezing between two of them. One nearly ran her down, but it wasn't meant to be that way.

The ferry was in, waiting for her, only a few travellers left, most of them long gone home. She walked alone up the gangplank. She stood at the rail and she saw the city she was leaving behind, the tall buildings all alight and the dark harbour. She saw the scattering of people on the Opera House steps, soon they'd be coming in for the evening, all togged up, all the old ones with nothing better to do, and the young ones in love. And she thought of Hugh.

She thought of his face now, lined and puzzled, and the way he looked the first time she saw him, at the church there, and how she must have loved him from that moment on, without ever letting herself know it. And how it would be worth anything, all the world's suffering, if he'd held her to him once, and cried her name as he spent himself.

The boat sailed on, in waters calm then bumpy, with the shores rising and falling, and at last they were slowing, and at last they were in port. Her legs were able to carry her down the gangplank and over the concrete and past the fun park, quiet now and dark and deserted. When she lifted her eyes to the flat it was dark too, and silent. She crossed the road at the place she'd always crossed and went up the stairs, making the clap-clap she always made. She put her key into the lock and it fitted, as it always had.

The light sprang out to her touch. The mirror flashed back at her, as she passed it, and she went to the bedroom. And in the narrow space between the wardrobe and the corner of the room the gun was waiting for her, as she knew it would be.

Deirdre Kincaid picked it up firmly and ran her hands over the wood, then down the barrel. She saw Hugh at the party, pretending to aim it. She held it against her for a moment. She pulled the safety-catch back, then she walked to her chair. She put the muzzle in her mouth, and she pulled the trigger.